FENELLA MILLER

◆

A RELUCTANT BRIDE

Complete and Unabridged

LINFORD
Leicester

First published in Great Britain in 2009

First Linford Edition
published 2009

British Library CIP Data

Miller, Fenella
    A reluctant bride.—Large print ed.—
Linford romance library
1. Love stories
2. Large type books
I. Title
823.9'2 [F]

ISBN 978–1–84782–605–3

Published by
F. A. Thorpe (Publishing)
Anstey, Leicestershire

Set by Words & Graphics Ltd.
Anstey, Leicestershire
Printed and bound in Great Britain by
T. J. International Ltd., Padstow, Cornwall

This book is printed on acid-free paper

A RELUCTANT BRIDE

Persuaded by her mother to act as chaperone to her godmother's daughter, young widow Patience Sinclair doesn't realise quite what is involved. Lady Orpington is perfectly capable of arranging her daughter's come out, so why is Patience needed? But when she meets Lord Simon Orpington it all becomes perfectly clear. Their respective mothers intend them to make a match of it. And while Patience has no intention of marrying again, it seems that Simon has other ideas . . .

Books by Fenella Miller
in the Linford Romance Library:

THE RETURN OF LORD RIVENHALL
A COUNTRY MOUSE

1

Suffolk, 1812.

'Mama, please don't worry about me. I am perfectly happy living here with you. When dear Jack died at Talevera three years ago he left me with a comfortable income and a determination never to marry again.'

Lady Bryson shook her head, unconvinced by her daughter's protestations. 'My dear girl, you were married out of the cradle, the Major snatched you away from me before you had even a season. Good heavens, Patience, you are hardly in your dotage, you are only three and twenty and a beautiful young lady. It is high time you went back into society and found yourself another husband.'

Patience had heard quite enough of this nonsense recently. She pinned a smile to her face, pushing back a stray russet curl from her forehead.

'Mama, I have told you repeatedly that with Jack I had a perfect marriage.' She paused, her smile becoming sad. 'Of course, we were not blessed with children, but apart from that there is not a man on this earth who could match him. I shall not settle for second best.'

She watched her mother draw breath knowing she was about to embark on yet another reason why being a contented widow was not enough. 'Very well. As you are so insistent that I am mouldering away in this village I shall accept the invitation of my godmother and go and stay for the season at their London house.'

'My dear, I am so pleased to have changed your mind. Lady Orpington is not well and as her daughter Rosamond is to make her come out, she is in need of a companion for her.' The small, plump, lady jumped with surprising agility to her feet. 'I shall go at once and

2

write a letter to dear Eleanor and tell her that you are coming immediately.'

Patience laughed. 'I hope by your use of the word *immediately* you're referring to the writing of the letter and not my imminent departure to London?'

'You do not intend to go for the festive season? It is so quiet here; you would be much better enjoying yourself with people your own age. You have been out of black for more than two years it is high time you rejoined society.'

Patience was adamant. 'No, Mama, I shall stay here for Christmas and travel in the New Year. The season does not really start until March which should give me ample time to replenish my wardrobe and get to know Lady Rosamond.'

Lady Bryson accepted defeat. 'Well, my dear, I must own that I shall enjoy your company. I am sure that Eleanor will send her carriage for you so you may rest assured, your journey will be comfortable.'

'There is no need for that, Mama. I shall take the mail coach. As I shall be travelling with Mary and Sam Perkins, I shall come to no harm.'

'I can see that you have made up your mind so shall say no more about it. If you are travelling with a maid and a manservant you should be safe enough. I shall have the missive ready in thirty minutes. If you delay your ride until it is finished you could take it down to The Red Lion for me.'

Patience agreed to wait until the letter was done. She had been about to take her huge black gelding for a gallop through the woods whilst the weather was clement and was already dressed in a handsome, green riding-habit that exactly matched the colour of her eyes. She tapped her booted foot on the carpet feeling decidedly put out.

When she had returned to live with her mother in the comfortable Dower House, she had thought she would never recover from the loss of her dear friend and husband. She had spent four years following the drum and had loved every moment of it. She had nursed wounded officers and even delivered a baby. Her life had been full of excitement and wherever the regiment had gone, she had been there.

The widow of a common soldier was often remarried before her husband was cold in his grave for she would have been unable to stay in camp on her own. The wife of the commanding officer, as her husband had been by then, did not have such an option. She was obliged to make her way home with Mary and Sam to recover slowly in the peace of the Suffolk countryside.

Now she was obliged to spend several months in London escorting a young debutante, of seventeen years, to various routs, soirees and balls. She frowned, shuddering at the thought of being constrained to make polite small talk to other matrons and companions. She thanked God that as a widow she would not be required to join in the jollity and dancing.

She spun and paced the room, ending in front of the gilt mantle-glass. At least she could put on her hat whilst she waited. She stared at her reflection in the mirror her head to one side. Her mother was right, she seemed to have grown into her looks since she had returned to England. She had lost the roundness of youth and her spectacular emerald eyes appeared to dominate the oval of her face.

This would not do. The last thing she required was to be admired by members of the *ton*. She was not wealthy, not by her godmother's standards, but she was comfortable and owned a neat estate in Norfolk which brought her in more than enough for her modest monthly needs. She had not touched the money Jack had left her; indeed she had no idea how matters stood in that department. Her lips curved slightly. At least her visit to Town would enable her to see her lawyers.

She heard hurrying footsteps approaching the room. Good — her mother was returning with the letter. She pushed the final glass topped pin into her hat, collected her gloves and riding whip and went to meet her.

★ ★ ★

Grosvenor Square, London.

Lady Orpington put down the note from her oldest friend with a sigh of satisfaction. She looked across at the pretty, blonde girl curled up in a deep-seated chair, her nose firmly in the latest Gothic romance.

'Rosamond, my dear, Mrs Sinclair has agreed to join us and act as your companion. Is that not excellent news?'

The girl glanced up from her book, keeping her finger on the line she was reading. 'Mama, I do not see the necessity of employing a companion when you are quite capable of doing the job yourself.'

'I have told you my health has been a trifle uncertain of late and I should hate to ruin your come out by being unable to accompany you. And the thought of organising your ball is too fatiguing. And Mrs Sinclair is not an employee; she will be an honoured guest. She has agreed to help me out of the kindness of her heart because I am her godmother.'

'Have you asked Simon if he minds?'

'Your brother might be the head of the family, but I am his mother and I do not have to ask permission to invite my goddaughter to stay. She was married to Colonel Sinclair, a hero of the Peninsula, for several years and has been a widow for three. Simon will hardly consider her arrival as a threat to his freedom.'

Rosamond giggled, her blonde ringlets bouncing around her heart-shaped face. 'I hope that you are correct, Mama. Remember he threatened to send you to moulder at his estate in Hertfordshire if you attempted any more matchmaking.'

'Matchmaking? If I had any such

notion in mind, I should not be looking in the direction of a widow who had spent her entire married life racketing all over Portugal and Spain. But, dear Simon, *is* the last of the line and he will be thirty on his next name day. It is high time he set up his nursery.'

'And so you tell him almost every time he dares to venture into our side of the house.' She yawned, tossing her book aside. 'Anyway, I am delighted she is coming; it will be lovely to have someone nearer my own age to talk to. I am going to find myself another book at the circulating library. Would you like to come with me?'

'No, thank you, I wish to speak to Cook about the menus for next week.' Lady Orpington called her daughter back. 'Rosamond, would you be so kind as to pull the bell strap for me? I shall ask Bentley to convey a message to Simon. He should have finished dressing by now.'

'It rather depends on exactly what time he returned home last night. Now

Parliament is no longer in session he has no reason to rise early.'

'In that case I shall be sure to find him in his apartments.'

* * *

Simon, Lord Orpington, a peer of the realm, scowled at his valet. 'Good grief! Another bear-garden jaw from my dear mother. I wonder what it is I have done to offend her delicate sensibilities this time.'

'Lady Rosamond was laughing when she left the drawing room so I doubt you have anything to worry about, my lord.'

Simon relaxed a little. It never failed to astonish him how the servants always knew what any of them were doing. 'I am relieved to hear that. No, my stock will do. I shall go directly to Lady Orpington; I am intrigued as to why I have had such an urgent summons.'

His valet stood aside, allowing him to

stand, before holding out his navy blue superfine coat. As Simon shrugged his way into the garment he caught a glimpse of himself reflected in the tall window. He drew in his stomach and squared his shoulders. Was he letting himself go? Did he no longer have the musculature of an athlete?

When he had been forced to return from his position with the Duke of Wellington, on the death, four years previously, of both his brother and father, he had been battle hard. His wits were as sharp as his sword. He feared the life he was living was not conducive to a healthy body. He must consider his options. His estates were well run in his absence, but would be even better if he spent more than a week or so in residence.

He was bored. He found civilian life flat and even the cut and thrust of debate in the House of Lords could not replace the excitement of his time as an aid to Wellington. He sighed. There was nothing he could do about matters, he could not rejoin his regiment, he had responsibilities. He was the last of his line as his dear mama kept reminding him.

'I shall be back before I go out, Roberts. I shall need my driving coat.'

He strode from the room ignoring the two footmen who leapt to attention as he passed. He had not spoken to his mother for several days which was remiss of him. His rooms were situated on the right of the grand entrance hall his mother and sister occupied the rest of the house. He paused outside the drawing room waiting for the butler, Bentley, to hurry forward and open the doors.

He smiled as he saw his mother dozing in front of the fire. He loved her dearly and if only she would refrain from mentioning matrimony every time he appeared at her side, he would visit her more often.

'Mama, you wish to see me?'

Not at all discommoded by being found asleep in front of the fire Lady Orpington smiled warmly at her remaining son.

'I have asked for coffee to be served as soon as you joined me.' She patted the space next to her on the sofa. 'Please, Simon, come and sit here. There is something I wish to ask you.'

His heart sunk and he wished he had not been so eager to call. He knew what was coming; she had another hopeful young debutante to throw at his head. Would she never learn? He had no intention of getting leg-shackled in the foreseeable future and certainly not to any of the whey faced, simpering schoolgirls his mother appeared to think suitable to be the next countess.

'I cannot stay long, I am sorry, Mama, I have an appointment elsewhere.' He strolled to the window and perched himself in the deep embrasure. He crossed his long, booted legs at the ankles, frowning as he detected a speck of dust on the toe.

'You need not look so cross, my dear; I do not break my promises. I have not asked you here to discuss anything you should dislike.'

Simon felt an unpleasant heat colour his cheeks and his stock felt unaccountably tight. 'I apologise, Mama; I should be delighted to have some coffee with you.' He walked over to join her, loving the way she accepted his apology without comment. 'Well, what is it you wish to ask me?' Whatever it was he knew, after his rudeness, he would be inclined to agree.

'I have invited my goddaughter, Mrs Sinclair, to oversee your sister's come out. She was married for several years to Colonel Sinclair but sadly he was killed at Talevera. Her mother, my dearest friend, Lady Bryson, has been worried about her daughter. It is three years since she was made a widow and Lady Bryson believes it is high time Mrs Sinclair rejoined the world. By asking her to help with Rosamond I am assisting both Lady Bryson and myself. I was rather dreading having to organise the ball. And you know what your sister is like, she will wish to attend every party that she is invited to, as well as attending the opera and theatre. My heart sinks at the very thought of all that activity.'

'I met Colonel Sinclair once. He was a good man. I think it is an excellent idea, you have my full approval. When is Mrs Sinclair coming to join us?'

'Not until after the festive season; she wishes to spend Christmas at home, but she will be here in the New Year.'

The coffee tray arrived and the conversation turned to other topics. When Simon left to return to his own domain he had almost forgotten why he had been summoned. The arrival of Colonel Sinclair's widow was of no interest to him. She must be in her thirties, Sinclair had been at least ten years his senior. For once he was in full agreement with his mother. Rosamond could be a handful, having an older friend would be a steadying influence on her.

★　★　★

In the drawing room his mother was equally satisfied with the encounter.

She had not exactly misled her son, merely allowed him to assume that dear Patience was ten years older than she actually was. She smiled. This time she truly believed she had found exactly the right person for her finicky son for if anyone had been misnamed it was the auburn haired, green-eyed, fiery tempered Patience Sinclair.

2

The mail coach rattled into the yard of the London coaching inn. Patience sighed with relief. The two-day journey had become wearisome; her initial enthusiasm for the novelty had evaporated by the end of the first day. Although their accommodation had been adequate, indeed far better than many places she had been obliged to stay in on the continent, her chamber had been facing the yard and the noise had kept her awake.

She turned to her companions, Sam and Mary Perkins. 'At last. We have arrived at our destination. Sam could you find a hackney carriage for us and oversee the removal of the trunks from the coach? Mary, you and I shall go inside and freshen up.'

'Right away, madam. Shall you be wanting to leave directly for Grosvenor

Square?' Sam asked as he handed his employer from the vehicle.

'Yes, Sam. The sooner we arrive the better. I should like to be able to see the house I am to live in for the next four months and it will be dark in an hour or so.'

Patience discovered that the inside of the hostelry was as busy as the yard. There were no private parlours available but the landlady kindly allowed them the use of a bedchamber in order to wash their faces. Twenty minutes later they were summoned back downstairs to complete the final stage of the journey from Ipswich.

'I had forgotten how evil-smelling a big city can be, even in the depths of winter.' Patience said smiling. 'One must pray that Grosvenor Square is more salubrious than this area or I shall be returning home long before the end of the season.'

Mary nodded sympathetically. 'I reckon as you've got out of the habit of travelling, madam. Why, a few years back you and the Colonel wouldn't have turned a hair at the noise and odour.'

'I am afraid that you are right, Mary. Mama was correct to insist that I accepted this invitation. It is a poor thing when a woman of only three and twenty becomes as set and staid in her ways as a widow of twice that age.'

'Well, madam, you might feel like an older lady but in that travelling outfit you look like a young lady of fashion.'

Patience glanced down at her fur-trimmed pelisse in a fetching shade of plum. 'I own that this is an attractive ensemble. We are lucky to have such a good seamstress available to us in the village. I believe that this design came from one of the most recent pages of *La Belle Assemble*.'

She pulled the travelling rug closer around her knees. In spite of the windows being firmly closed it was cold enough in the coach for ice to form on the inside of the windows. She leant back against the squabs and closed her eyes, allowing her mind to drift back to the last time she had bounced over cobbles in the cold.

Her eyes filled with tears as she recalled her journey back from Spain after dear Jack had been killed. She had vowed then, never to venture abroad again. Her travelling days were over; she would return to Ipswich and live the quiet life she had spurned in her youth. She would be a devoted aunt to her older brother's many progeny and a loving daughter to her widowed mother.

And this she had done for the past three years, but she had to admit that she was a trifle bored by the unalloyed tranquillity of the countryside. She had attended the theatre at Ipswich and a variety of entertainments in the homes of the local gentry, but interesting company was sparse and she was starved of intelligent conversation. She doubted she would find much to stimulate the intellect at the vapid parties of the *ton* but at least she could return home in June with fresh memories and a trunkful of new books.

The road became smoother and the shouts and cries of street vendors and the press of unwashed humanity were left behind as the carriage entered the more refined area of the city. Patience scrubbed a clear space on the frosty window with her gloved hand in order to look out.

'These houses are very fine, are they not, Mary? And I am glad to see that the pavements are swept clean and that both ladies and gentlemen are promenading safely.'

'You'll miss your riding, madam. Shall you hire a riding hack whilst you're here?'

'I am hoping that there will be something suitable in the stables. Lord Orpington was a cavalry officer so I am certain he will have a large selection of excellent mounts available.'

The carriage slowed its progress and pulled up in front of an imposing three-storey, stucco townhouse. The house was detached from its neighbours by an archway on either side of the building. A handsome flight of white marble steps led up to the front door.

Sam, who had travelled on top with the jarvey, let down the steps and opened the door. As Patience alighted the front door swung open and a virtual regiment of uniformed footmen poured out. She stiffened. Surely all this pomp was not in her honour? As a black garbed, silver haired gentlemen hurried down the steps to greet her she realised that it was.

The butler bowed deeply. 'Welcome to Orpington House, Mrs Sinclair. It is an honour to have you with us. I am Bentley, at your service. The house-keeper, Mrs Ridgeway, is waiting to escort you to your apartment if you would care to follow me?'

Patience knew enough about etiquette in high society not to make the mistake of thanking this august gentle-men. She merely nodded her head, picked up her skirts, and did as she was bid. She paused halfway up the steps to look around with interest, for after all this was to be her home for the next few months.

So far she was favourably impressed. The house was well-kept and the footmen well-fed, a sign, she believed, of a happy house. Bentley bowed her in. She looked round the vast marble floored entrance hall with wide eyes. An elegant flight of stairs ran up either side and a handsome carved wooden gallery over-looked the space in which she stood. She noticed the numerous passageways and doors and feared she would need a guide to find her way around.

'Mrs Sinclair, this is the housekeeper, Mrs Ridgeway. She will conduct you upstairs and answer any questions. Lady Orpington and Lady Rosamond have asked if you would care to join them for afternoon tea at 4 o'clock. Dinner is served at seven.'

Patience smiled. 'Please convey my thanks to Lady Orpington and tell her that I should be delighted to join her for afternoon tea.'

She followed the rigid back of the housekeeper up the left hand flight of stairs. Mrs Ridgeway had curtsied, but the gesture had been minimal. Why was the housekeeper not happy about her arrival? She was to find out as a footman opened the door to her new accommodation.

'This is your apartment, Mrs Sinclair. It is a pity that your luggage did not arrive ahead of you. I should like to have had everything clean and pressed.'

Patience hid her smile. Obviously travelling by mail coach and not accepting the offer of the family carriage for her journey had put her beyond the pale. Too bad! She would be beholden to no one. She was an independent woman, made her own decisions and not even the disapproval of such a personage as Mrs Ridgeway was going to change that.

'My abigail will soon have things sorted to my satisfaction, Mrs Ridgeway. I shall require the services of a chambermaid whilst I am staying here.

Also I hope you have arranged for my man, Perkins and his wife to have shared accommodation?'

This is obviously something else that rankled with the hatchet faced housekeeper. 'We do not employ married staff, Mrs Sinclair, at Orpington House. Female staff have their rooms in the attics and male staff above the stables. I have made rooms available in each place for your servants.'

Patience could not believe her ears. This woman, a mere housekeeper, had the temerity to insist that Sam and Mary should spend the next four months apart. She would not have it, but knew better than to argue with a servant. Ignoring the housekeeper she turned to Mary, hovering anxiously in the passageway, waiting for the explosion from her mistress.

'Mary, let us go in and explore the rooms.' She spoke with her back to the housekeeper. 'That will be all, Ridgeway.' She deliberately dropped the courtesy title, making it clear that the matter of the accommodation was not over.

'What a pretty room, and so warm.' She looked round in delight at the sitting room she was to have exclusive use of for the next few months. A large fireplace held a roaring fire; placed adjacent to it were two deep-seated, damask covered armchairs and a matching *chaise-longue*. The polished boards were covered by delightful flowered rugs.

'Look, Mary, I have an *escritoire* and a sewing table. I do believe all these pieces of furniture have been made by Sheraton. I had no idea that Orpington was so warm. It is no wonder my mother says he is the most eligible *parti* in town.'

She heard the door close behind her and knew the objectionable house-keeper had taken her leave. She glanced over her shoulder to check before speaking again.

'Please do not worry, Mary, I shall organise rooms for you and Sam when I speak to Lady Orpington. It is possible that you will have to sleep apart initially but I can assure you that it will not be for more than a night or two.'

'Don't fret, madam. My Sam and I can survive being separated. Please don't make a fuss on our behalf. I'd not want you to upset Lady Orpington so soon.'

Patience laughed. 'I shall try to behave. I promised myself that I would curb my temper and be the perfect guest. So please do not look so worried; we shall not be evicted today.'

Sam directed the unloading of the trunks and within ten minutes of their arrival they were safely stowed in the enormous closet that led from her commodious bedchamber. Mrs Ridgeway sent not one, but two chambermaids to wait on Patience. She left the direction of these girls to Mary, knowing that in a very short space of time her garments and toiletries would be organised.

When the appointed hour arrived she had taken a quick bath in the room adapted specially for that purpose and was freshly dressed in a becoming afternoon gown of daffodil yellow. The prevailing fashion of high waists admirably suited her tall, slender form and emphasised her womanly curves. Mary had redressed her hair in a braided coronet. Patience believed it made her look older, more like a widow and less like a hopeful young woman on the lookout for another husband.

She was pleased to discover a footman stationed outside her parlour door. The young man grinned. 'Mr Bentley said I was to take you down to the drawing room.'

'That was thoughtful of him.' Patience followed the young man along the spacious corridor, past the rows of grim faced ancestors hanging on the walls, and this time they used the right hand staircase. She assumed that one side was for ascending the other to descend. They crossed the chilly expanse of marble and the young man knocked loudly on the double doors on the far side.

The hall was lit by hundreds of

candles and a huge log fire cast a welcome warmth throughout the space. She was enchanted and was prepared to forget the unpleasant housekeeper if the rest of the staff, and the premises, were as warm and welcoming as the hall.

The footman announced her and she stepped in to be greeted by shrieks of delight and a flurry of sprigged muslin as Lady Rosamond ran across the room to embrace her.

'Mrs Sinclair, I cannot say how pleased I am to meet you. You are so beautiful and scarcely older than I am.'

Patience was a head taller than the girl who held her hands. 'Lady Rosamond, I am delighted to make your acquaintance. And thank you for your compliments. However, I believe that your fair beauty easily eclipses mine.'

The girl, still clutching her hands, led her across to meet Lady Orpington.

'Welcome, my dear, you are even lovelier than I remember. Come and sit beside me and give me all your news.'

Patience curtsied politely and allowed

Rosamond to guide her to the appointed place. By the time she had told her godmother everything about her life it was almost time to retire to her rooms to dress for dinner.

'Orpington will be joining us tonight in honour of your arrival. I do not believe that you have ever met. He was abroad when you married and he told us that, although he had met Colonel Sinclair, he had never had the pleasure of meeting you.'

Patience spent longer than usual selecting her evening gown. Finally she settled on an emerald green silk with a gold sarcenet overskirt. It had elbow length sleeves and a modest décolletage.

'Madam, I beg you, please do not wear a cap. You are far too young to adopt such an article even if you are a widow.'

Patience smiled ruefully. 'I must admit that with this gown it would look rather silly. I wish I had insisted that the modiste had made me a matching turban.'

'I thank the Lord that you didn't.' Mary shook out the folds of the skirt and handed Patience the small ribbon attached to the back of her gown which held her demi-train from under her feet. 'Are you going to take the matching reticule?'

'No, I do not think I need a bag tonight. I shall not be late, Mary. I am fatigued after the journey and require an early night. Tomorrow I intend to explore the house and gardens, familiarise myself with my new home. I must apologise that I have not managed to overturn the ruling about your accommodation. I intend to speak to Lord Orpington tonight about the matter.'

* * *

Downstairs Simon, formidable in black evening dress, favouring pantaloons and slippers over britches and silk stockings, waited in the drawing room to meet Colonel Sinclair's relict. His mother and sister had not come down; this was not unusual for they were infamous for their tardy arrivals.

He frowned. He sincerely hoped he would not be obliged to entertain Mrs Sinclair on his own. His fund of small talk was as limited as his temper. He straightened; he could hear the sound of female footsteps crossing the marble floor. He pinned a polite smile on his handsome face and ran his hand through his short dark hair, inadvertently ruffling it and making him look decidedly rakish.

The door opened and the footman announced Mrs Sinclair. Simon stepped forward to greet his guest. He halted and his jaw hardened. Was this some kind of joke? Who was this ravishing young woman? For it certainly could not be the middle-aged widow of Colonel Sinclair.

3

Patience walked into the drawing room knowing she looked her best. She was somewhat taken aback to find that neither Lady Orpington nor her daughter were present. Lord Orpington was alone. She hesitated. Should she go in unchaperoned? It was too late; she was committed as the footman announced her.

She dropped gracefully into a curtsy and, straightening, raised her head to meet the eyes of her host. She swallowed nervously. Why was the decidedly attractive gentleman staring at her with narrowed eyes? Had she a smut upon her nose? What could she possibly have done to offend him so early in her visit?

The earl bowed his head a fraction but made no attempt to take her hand. She bristled. He might be a peer of the realm but he had no manners. 'I bid you good evening, my lord.' She waited for his response but it was not forthcoming. He continued to stare at her with what could only be called a supercilious sneer on his lips.

This would not do — it would not do at all. She was obliged to remain under his roof for months and had no intention of being treated with disdain by anyone, however top lofty they might consider themselves to be.

Head high, green eyes flashing dangerously, she strode towards him. To her consternation he remained where he was. She had expected him to retreat, giving her the ascendancy. Instead she was forced to halt a scant pace from a man who emanated power and dislike in equal quantities.

'My lord, I had no wish to be at daggers drawn with you. I have come here at the insistence of Lady Orpington in order to act as companion to your sister on her come out. If you are concerned that I propose to replenish my wardrobe at your expense, you may rest assured that I intend to pay my own way. I am an independent woman, beholden to no one.'

She glared at him, refusing to be intimidated. She realised he was a foot taller than herself and she had always thought herself to be a beanpole. She saw a flicker of something that might have been admiration cross his face before he spoke.

'I must apologise, madam, if I appeared less than welcoming. I am, of course, delighted that you accepted my mother's invitation. As I have no intention of trailing after my sister during the season, it is fortunate that you are here to keep my mother company.'

Patience noticed that he made no reference to her rather vulgar remark about the cost of her garments. 'You will attend the ball to be held here, Lord Orpington? It would seem rather odd if you did not appear at your own sister's come out.'

She saw him grinding his teeth and knew he was having difficulty controlling his temper. Good! If he was rude to her then she would be entirely in the right!

'Naturally I shall attend the ball here. What I do not intend to do is accompany Rosamond to Almack's.'

'I do not blame you, my lord. From what I hear it sounds a dismal place. Nothing decent to drink and the supper is no better. I do not know why the debutantes are not paraded around a ring like the horses at Newmarket and be done with it.'

His sudden bark of laughter startled them both. 'Mrs Sinclair, you are an original! But I would respectfully suggest that you keep your opinion of the marriage mart to yourself.'

Lady Orpington and Rosamond arrived at that moment and Patience was almost disappointed that her tête-à-tête with the irascible lord was over. She smiled politely at her hostess.

'My dear Patience, we really must

apologise for arriving late. But I see that Simon and you have got acquainted. That is a beautiful dress, my dear, one could hardly credit that it was made by a country modiste.'

'Thank you, Lady Orpington. I fear that I am eclipsed by both you and Lady Rosamond. Your gold-silk gown is exquisite. I particularly like the way your turban and the egret feathers exactly match.' She gestured towards Rosamond who was eagerly awaiting the compliments she knew must come her way.

'White and silver gauze are a perfect combination for you, Lady Rosamond. And the silver ribbons threaded through your hair compliment your ensemble perfectly.'

The girl preened and twirled on the spot, making the dress fly out around her ankles, revealing silver stockings with matching heeled slippers. 'It is the first time that Mama has allowed me to wear this. It is in your honour. All my evening gowns have to be in silver or white. Some might consider this to be tiresome, but I believe that my hair goes well with the palest colours.'

There was no time for further mutual admiration as Bentley opened the doors at the far end of the elegant drawing room to announce that dinner was served. Patience could not fail to be aware that his lordship joined little in the conversation, his expression bland, his intelligent eyes watchful. He made no effort to entertain either her or the other members of the party. If she was honest, she had to admit that he blatantly ignored her.

It was with some relief that she followed Lady Orpington and her daughter back to the drawing room, allowing his lordship to consume his port in solitary splendour. She could feel the beginnings of a megrim hovering over her right eye. She curtsied to Lady Orpington.

'I beg that you will excuse me, I have the headache and must retire to my room if I'm not to be prostrate for a day or more. I do not often get a sick headache, but I fear that tonight is going to be one of those unfortunate occasions.'

Lady Orpington was immediately concerned. 'Poor thing! I suffer from them myself. It has been a long day and I expect you are overtired. A good night's sleep will hopefully restore you by the morning. Run along, my dear, I shall make your apologies to Simon when he joins us.'

'Thank you. It is my intention to ride before breakfast every morning. Is there a suitable mount I may borrow in the stable?'

Lord Orpington answered her question. 'You are welcome to ride anything in my stable, Mrs Sinclair. Jonah, the head groom, will be happy to assist your choice and accompany you.'

Where had the wretched man come from? He certainly had not entered the drawing room from the far end. She hoped he did not make a habit of creeping up behind a person scaring them half to death. From a man of his height and build he was remarkably soft footed.

She smiled her thanks. 'That is a generous offer you, my lord. However my man, Sam Perkins, goes everywhere with me. He and his wife followed my husband and I throughout our years on the continent.' Now was the ideal opportunity to mention the sleeping accommodation but her head pounded so painfully she did not have the energy to raise the subject. 'If you will excuse me, my lord, I have the headache.'

She did not wait to hear his reply but turned and hurried from the room. The ever attentive young footman was waiting to light her to her bedchamber.

'I have been assigned to you for your stay, Mrs Sinclair. Anything you want fetching or carrying, just ask for Harry.' He grinned. 'That's me, madam.'

'Thank you, Harry. I shall not require you any more this evening. Goodnight.'

Mary was waiting to help her disrobe. 'Is your head bad, madam?

Shall I fetch you a tisane from the kitchen?' She had known her young mistress since the cradle and could recognise the signs almost before Patience could herself.

'I want nothing else, thank you, apart from to get my head down on the cool pillows. Could you lay out my green riding habit for tomorrow morning and tell Sam I shall require his presence in the stable yard at dawn?'

'I shall certainly tell him to be ready, but not to be surprised if you don't appear.' The maid slipped a warm cotton night-rail over Patience's head. 'There you are. I shall leave a basin on the bedside table in case you feel poorly in the night.'

'What should I do without you and Sam, Mary? You are more dear to me than anyone, apart from my family.'

★ ★ ★

The mantle clock chimed six. Patience scrambled out of bed delighted to discover that her headache had cleared and she felt fully restored. The glow from the fire place gave her sufficient light to dress in her habit. Using a spill to light a candle she was ready to find her way downstairs and out to the stable.

Although it was early and not yet light, already the great house was astir. She was obliged to step round two maids on their knees, sacks tied around for aprons, their wooden pails full of sudsy water, scrubbing the marble floor in the hall. Footmen were equally busy dusting and polishing the panelling on the walls.

Harry, her own personal footman, appeared at her side, his wig slightly askew and his smart blue jacket incorrectly buttoned. 'You should have rung for me, Mrs Sinclair. It is my job to escort you around the house.'

'I did not expect you to be up so early, Harry. However, I am delighted to see you because you can conduct me to the stables.' She grinned. 'After you have adjusted your clothing, of course.'

Hastily he pushed his white half-wig on as it should be and re-buttoned his gold-frogged coat. 'Thank you, madam. Mr Bentley would have fined me a day's pay if he'd seen me like that.'

Patience smiled, well pleased that her kindness had secured the young man's devotion. Having ears and eyes below stairs in another's house was always useful.

Outside it was dark — but not inky black, more dark grey; dawn would not be long coming. She increased her pace, forcing the footman to run in order to keep up with her. 'I want to get off before anyone is around.' She knew it was not necessary to inform a servant of ones reasons but she had always found that they were far more co-operative if one did so.

'The stables are under that archway, Mrs Sinclair.'

'Excellent. I can find my own way from here. I shall send for you on my return, never fear, for I am certain that

I should be lost in a moment without your help.'

The stables were still locked up, the top doors of the loose boxes closed. She could hear the animals stamping and snorting impatiently, knowing that it would soon be the end of their nighttime incarceration. Sam was waiting for her.

'I took the liberty of lighting the lanterns, ma'am. Black as your hat down here without them.'

'I am glad that you did so for I wish to see what manner of horseflesh I have to choose from. Where shall we start opening?'

'I reckon the best of the bunch will be in boxes directly under the grooms' accommodation. They'd want to hear if there was anything untoward going on.'

Patience almost ran to the block of stables Sam was referring to. As she reached up to unbolt the first door an enormous hoof smashed against the wood. She laughed. 'This sounds like the one I want to ride.' She loved a horse with the fire to match her own.

She had more sense than to stand directly in front of the opening door. Instead she used the wood as a shield, pulling the half-door wide whilst peering round with interest. A huge chestnut head snaked out, teeth barred, ears flat to his head. Laughing at his antics she reached round and grabbed the angry animal's top lip and twisted gently.

Holding tight she emerged from her hiding place, crooning softly to the stallion. Sam watched as she worked her magic. He saw the animal's ears flick forwards and the bunched muscles on his massive neck relaxed.

'There now, silly boy. I am not going to hurt you. Let me stroke your face.' Slowly Patience released his mouth and transferred her hand to his nose, rubbing gently, and breathing into his flared nostrils. 'He is calm now, Sam. Find his tack — I doubt this magnificent gentleman will have a side saddle so astride it shall have to be.'

Sam glanced up at the inscription above the door. Rufus — a good name for a chestnut horse. He didn't question his mistresses order knowing that her habit had a cleverly divided skirt which made riding either side saddle or astride possible without displaying unseemly expanses of leg.

Patience unbolted the lower door and slipped inside with the handsome beast. She was fizzing with excitement at the thought of riding him. She knew Rufus must be the mount of his lordship, but it made no odds. He had given her permission to ride any horse she wanted and she wanted this one. She took hold of the dangling end of his leather halter and led him round to the manager knowing there would be a hook to fasten him to.

Ten minutes later Rufus, and the rangy bay gelding Sam had selected, were tacked and ready to go. Patience gathered up the double reins and crooked her leg for Sam to toss her into the saddle. Rufus skittered nervously, unused to such a light weight on his back. She spoke soothingly to him and he calmed.

'I hope you know the way to the park, Sam. I should hate to get lost and find myself out in broad daylight sitting astride a man's mount in fashionable London. My reputation would be shredded and I would be packed home in disgrace.'

What her servant thought of her decision to ride Lord Orpington's favourite, he was wise to keep to himself. He knew from bitter experience that criticism goaded Miss Patience on to worse behaviour. It was best to leave her to get the devilment out of her system.

★   ★   ★

Lord Orpington had no such scruples. The entire stable and a considerable distance beyond heard exactly what he thought of a young woman who had the audacity to borrow his finest horse for the use of her man servant. If he had known the real truth the air would have been blue.

★ ★ ★

It was hardly light when Patience and Sam clattered back into the stables. A stable boy jumped forward to take her reins but for some reason wouldn't meet her eye. A flicker of unease passed through her — surely Orpington hadn't discovered that she had borrowed his stallion? Lady Orpington had informed her last night that her son was going to his club after dinner which should have meant that he would not rise from his bed until noon.

Not waiting for Sam to help her dismount, she vaulted from the saddle and headed for the house. Pulling off her gloves as she went, she arrived at the side entrance just as Harry stepped out from the shadows to speak urgently to her.

'His lordship is in a fair old rage, ma'am. He got up early to ride and discovered that you had taken his mount. He's steaming up and down the passageway waiting to catch you as you go in.'

'Oh dear! I have no wish to speak to him until I've bathed and changed. Is there another way?'

'You could go in the boot room door and up the back stairs. But we've got to make sure Mr Bentley don't catch us.'

Patience reached the sanctuary of her bed-chamber and was on her way back down stairs in less than twenty minutes. Now she was dressed in a fetching pale-green promenade dress with matching spencer. It also had a pretty poke bonnet and reticule to complete the ensemble, but she rather thought appearing as if she was about to go out would enrage her irascible host even more.

'Harry, where is Lord Orpington?'

'His lordship's in his study, Mrs Sinclair; but no-one ever disturbs him there.'

'Kindly direct me to this room.'

He led her along several impressively

wide passage ways and halted in front of a solid door. She nodded, unable to speak as her heart was somewhere in the region of her throat. She was more fearful than when she had waited behind the lines for a battle to commence. She stiffened her backbone, chiding herself for being faint-hearted in the face of the enemy.

'There is no need to announce me, Harry.' She took a deep calming breath and knocked loudly on the door.

'Enter.' The shouted command did nothing to reassure her.

Her hand was shaking so much she could hardly turn the smooth glass knob. She pushed open the door and stepped in, head high, waiting for the world to fall down upon her head.

4

Patience did not curtsey, she merely dipped her head, keeping her eyes fixed firmly on a point somewhere over Lord Orpington's left shoulder. She had no intention of allowing him to put her out of countenance with a basilisk stare. She moved gracefully into the room.

'You stole my horse, madam. What do you have to say for yourself?'

Shocked by his comment, she looked directly at him. She wished she had not. His icy stare sent shivers trickling down her spine. Her hands felt damp, her knees weak. She was obliged to swallow twice before finding her voice.

'My lord, I was under the distinct impression that you gave me leave to select whichever animal I chose from your stable. Naturally I chose the finest — your chestnut stallion is almost as good as my own horse, Othello.'

'Devil take it! Are you telling me that *you* rode Rufus — not your man?'

'Of course I did. Do you honestly believe I would give such an animal to my groom? That would be outrageous.'

He took two step towards her and she had to force herself not to retreat. 'What is outrageous, madam, is that you had the insolence to ride astride any horse. Good God — I have a reputation to protect — I will not have you gallivanting all over the place dressed in man's attire like a Spanish peasant.'

Patience was no longer scared. She was furious. How dare this man, a total stranger, speak to her as if she was a child? No, worse — a servant. Twin spots of red gave due warning of what was to come.

'How dare you use that tone with me, Orpington? I am neither a dependent nor a servant and will not stand for it. I shall send for my own horse if you do not wish me to ride one from your stable, but I shall dress in whatever fashion *I* deem appropriate.'

She stared straight into his eyes, which were darkened by fury to almost black. She could see his throat muscles moving, his fists bunching, and knew in that second, that she had seriously mistaken her opponent. He was no gentleman — he was going to physically retaliate for her rudeness.

She was brave, but not stupid. Before his hands could grasp her arms she skipped backwards, picked up her skirt and fled from the room. She kicked the door shut then froze not sure in which direction to go. Endless corridor stretched either way — which one led to safety?

*   *   *

Simon's fists slowly uncurled as he stared at the empty space that had seconds before held his quarry. He was tempted to pursue her but sanity prevailed. With a sudden roar of frustration he spun and swept the items from the top of his desk on to the floor.

The resulting crash of broken glass and ruined books did something to restore his equanimity.

Mrs Sinclair had not been in the household a day and already he had lost his temper — twice. He could not recall the last time he had been so angry. Nobody had ever confronted him in that manner. They had more sense. His knotted shoulder muscles relaxed and he was once more in control.

He surveyed the chaos he had caused with a rueful smile. It was years since he had behaved like a petulant schoolboy. What was it about that woman which brought out the worst in him? He was smiling as he turned to pull the bell strap to summon a footman to clear up. His hand stopped inches from the velvet tassel. God in his heaven! If the girl had not fled he would have struck her. He had never raised his hand to a woman. It was not the behaviour of gentleman, it was unpardonable.

His hands began to shake, as if with

an ague, as the enormity of his behaviour registered. He had not only accused a guest in his house of stealing his horse but also of behaving like a Spanish peasant. No wonder her magnificent green eyes had flashed defiance.

He distinctly remembered, now he was calm, telling her she could have the pick of the stable. Of course he had not realised she would take his favourite stallion, but she had not done anything wrong. It was he who was monstrously at fault.

He was famous for his *sang-froid*, all it ever took for him to depress a person's pretensions was a curled lip or a slight rise of an aristocratic eyebrow. His friends would not believe he had been within a hair's breadth of beating a female. Indeed he could hardly believe it himself. He had a deal of fence-mending to do and dithering in his study was not the place to do it.

He would sally forth and find Mrs Sinclair and make her the most grovelling of apologies. The fact that his appalling behaviour had played right into both her hands, and his matchmaking mother's, served him right. As soon as he had set eyes on the beautiful young woman he had known his mother had tricked him. He would never have agreed to her visit if he had known she was not a dried up, middle aged woman, firmly on the shelf. She was another hopeful candidate for the vacant position of countess.

Simon glanced into one of the pier gilt mirrors that hung on either side of the handsome window. His normally immaculate appearance was somewhat disarrayed; his stock was rumpled and his hair out of place. Hastily he remedied the damage and strode across the Brussels carpet and flung open the door. For the second time that morning he was nonplussed.

*　*　*

Patience ran to the left only to be faced by two more long, empty corridors and not a friendly footman in sight to direct her. She wished she had paid more attention when Harry had led her into Lord Orpington's domain, but she had been too anxious to take note of her surroundings. None of it looked familiar. In fact any one of the doors could be the sleeping quarters of her host.

She felt herself colour from toes to the crown of her head at the thought of being discovered by anyone, even the friendly Harry, lurking around this forbidden area. Orpington had said *his* reputation would be damaged by her riding astride, but *she* would be totally ruined if word was to get out that she was wandering alone, unchaperoned by even a maid, in this strictly male part of Orpington House.

She had no choice. She would have to return to the study and pray that the formidable earl had recovered his temper. Why had she been so impulsive? She had thought that this trait had been firmly squashed over her years of marriage and widowhood.

At her birth her father had taken one look at her screaming, red-faced and furious, moments after her birth, her fiery red hair exactly like his own and insisted that she be called Patience. If ever a child had been misnamed it was her. In spite of frequent scoldings and occasional spanks she had spent her formative years tumbling from one scrape to another.

She smiled as she remembered meeting Jack Sinclair at a house party. It had been barely two weeks after her sixteenth birthday and she was scarcely out. She had been riding, alone, at dawn, when they had met. The rapport had been instant for both of them. He was twice her age and, like many military gentleman, felt matrimony was not for him. Meeting Patience had changed his mind.

The happy couple had been married by special license less than six weeks after their first meeting. The marriage had been happy from day one. Following the drum gave Patience all the excitement she craved and being the wife of a cavalry officer on active duty meant she had responsibilities and, for the first time in her life, was obliged to put others before herself. She learnt to curb her impulsive nature and was the perfect wife in every respect. She had been sad that no children had resulted from their union but relieved because Jack would have sent her home and that she could not have borne.

Now, in the space of twenty-four hours she had lost her temper twice. What was wrong with her? Maybe it would be better if she returned to the peace and quiet of the Suffolk countryside. She halted, for the second time that morning, outside the study door of Lord Orpington. Did she have the courage to knock? After all it had been barely ten minutes since she had run away from this very room.

As she raised her hand the door swung back and she found herself nose to nose with his lordship. Who was the more surprised it was difficult to tell.

Both recoiled; she retreated to the window on the far side of the passageway and he took two steps back into the safety of his room. From there they watched each other warily.

She could not tell if he was still enraged and was not sure whether it would be wiser to take to her heels again and pray that she met someone who could direct her out of the rabbit warren of rooms and corridors. To her astonishment he smiled. His eyes creased at the corners and he held out his hand to her.

'Please, Mrs Sinclair, do not hover over there. I promise I have recovered from my choler. It is quite safe to approach me.'

She found herself responding to his overture but remained where she was. Her heart returned to its normal place and her knees stopped wobbling. 'I realised that I should never find my way back to the entrance hall without assistance. Could you ring for someone to escort me back?'

'I shall take you myself. It is the least I can to after my abominable behaviour. I most humbly beg your pardon, madam, for losing my temper. I promise that it will never happen again, whatever the provocation.'

She moved closer. 'You were going to strike me, Lord Orpington.' It was not a question, it was a statement of fact. 'I am not accustomed to being threatened. A gentleman would not have done so.' As soon as the words were out of her mouth she regretted them. What had prompted her to say such a thing? A man such as he would not take slurs on his reputation kindly.

For a moment it hung in the balance. It could have gone either way. Then Simon laughed. 'Was that by way of a test, my dear? Did you wish to try my resolve not to lose my temper under any circumstances?'

She grinned, her eyes sparkling with devilment. 'I wish I could say it was, my lord. But I must admit that I spoke without thought, again. However, you have passed my unwitting test with flying colours. It is my turn to beg *your* pardon. I promise I shall do my best to guard my tongue in future.'

'I am delighted to hear you say so. From this point forward we shall be the best of friends.' It was his turn to swallow nervously.

His unthinking words could be misinterpreted. Before he knew where he was he could be leg shackled to this unpredictable, unconventional but undeniably beautiful young woman.

Patience had seen him hesitate and correctly interpreted his disquiet. 'I think we had better continue this conversation in the privacy of your study, my lord. I think there are several misunderstandings and they need to be resolved before we can deal comfortably together.'

She could sense his reluctance as he bowed and stepped aside to allow her to precede him into the room. He gestured towards the two comfortable armchairs set in front of the roaring fire and waited politely until she was settled before taking the other chair himself.

'My lord, I believe that we have both been duped. As soon as I met Lady Orpington I realised there was something havy-cavy going on. Your mama is no more unwell than I am. She has an admirable secretary and an efficient housekeeper. She has no need of my assistance to launch your sister in society next month.' She paused to gather her thoughts before continuing.

'My suspicions were aroused but it was not until I saw the look of incredulous horror when I stepped through the drawing room doors last night to realise the full extent of our parents' duplicity. We have been set up. We are being thrown together deliberately in the hope that we shall make a match of it.' She heard him shifting uncomfortably in his seat and knew she was not wrong.

She raised her head and gave him the full force of her smile. 'I have no intention of ever remarrying, my lord. I am, as I believe I have already told you, an independent woman. As a widow I have more freedom than I ever had as a wife or daughter. I have no intention of relinquishing that.' She watched him absorbing her words, realising he was not totally convinced that she had not been privy to the machinations.

'I shall be frank, my lord. The only reason I might consider matrimony was if I thought there was any prospect of having children of my own. But I was happily married for several years without producing offspring and must conclude that I am barren. Therefore I would be unsuitable as your countess and all we have to do is inform your mother of the facts and we shall both be safe.'

'Thank you for being so open, Mrs Sinclair. I shall be equally so with you. You are quite correct in your deduction — you were obviously invited here as a suitable bride. But I fear that my mother already knows the facts about your marriage and still considers you ideal.'

Patience frowned. 'Then she is wrong to do so. The whole purpose of the exercise would be for you to fill your nursery. Even I know that is the only reason you would give up your freedom. Why should she wish you to marry someone who cannot give you an heir?'

He hesitated before answering. 'I believe that our parents have decided that the fault did not lie with you but with the Colonel.'

Her mouth dropped open in shock as she understood what he was suggesting. Her darling husband had been unable to father children? How dare he cast aspersions on her beloved? She stormed to her feet.

'Whatever the truth of the matter, you may rest assured, my lord, that you would be the very last person I should choose to marry. If ever I relinquish my freedom it will be to a man of action, not a macaroni who idles his time away in frivolous pursuits.'

She swept from the room allowing

him no time to reply to her outrageous remarks.

⋆　⋆　⋆

Good grief! Simon was not sure whether to be offended or amused. He had been called many things in his life, but a macaroni? He was a Corinthian, a noted whipster and was famous for his elegance. He would rather be seen in his coffin than dressed in a violently striped waistcoat and a neck-cloth so high and starched that the wearer could not turn his head.

Chuckling he stood up. The gauntlet had been thrown. Another thing he was infamous for was never turning down a challenge.

5

The weather turned inclement and Patience found herself confined to the house with only Lady Orpington and Lady Rosamond for company. The mantua maker called and she was persuaded to order a ball gown and a fourth evening dress.

'You will need something special for my ball, Mrs Sinclair. It is to be the first of the season as Mama sent out the cards before Christmas to make sure that no one else secured the first Saturday after Easter.'

Patience hid her smile. It seemed there was no longer any pretence that she was here to help arrange this event. 'It is fortuitous, is it not, that Easter falls early this year. Imagine if you had had to wait until May for your big day?'

'The end of March is a trifle soon for the opening of the season,' Lady

Orpington commented. 'However, it means that people will not become overheated in the ballroom as they do at later events. Also we shall have dinner at six and start the ball at nine o'clock. One cannot rely on the weather in spring.'

'What theme are you having? Have you decided yet, Lady Rosamond?'

'I shall leave it until nearer the date. But, please would you call me Rosamond, using my title makes me feel so old?

'I should be delighted and you must call me Patience. I too have become tired of hearing myself addressed so formally.'

Lady Orpington smiled fondly at them. 'Perhaps you could call me Aunt Eleanor, my dear? For I am your godmother, after all.'

The matter was settled. Using familiar names made the atmosphere more relaxed and Patience finally began to think her journey had not been a waste of time and she might even come to enjoy herself. Cloistered in the Dower

House of Bryson Court with her mother, she had had no opportunity to mix with anyone her own age.

Her brother, Peter, was as different to her as chalk is from cheese. He was ten years her senior and where she was wit and sparkle he was sober and serious. His wife Amy had presented him with his first heir on their wedding anniversary. She had continued to produce another offspring for each year of their eight year marriage. Their nursery, at the Court, was full to overflowing.

She loved her many nieces and nephews and was always happy to take them out to play in the landscaped park, or drive them in her curricle, but her sister-in-law was too preoccupied with being a mother to have time for girlish chitchat.

Rosamond, six years her junior, was like a younger sister and within a short time they were bosom bows. Patience regaled her with an edited version of her life with the regiment and Rosamond shared her stories from her three years away at an exclusive seminary with the daughters of other wealthy aristocrats.

Patience was not sure if she was relieved, or disappointed, that Lord Orpington did not deign to appear at dinner again. She was assured by Aunt Eleanor that her son rarely dined at home, preferring to eat with his cronies at one or other of his clubs.

A little over a week after her arrival, Mary gave her the good news that the snow had gone and Sam would be expecting her in the stable the next morning. She went to her bed eagerly anticipating the treat of being able to ride again. She was bursting with energy and had missed expending it in one of her customary wild gallops. She wondered whether she would have the effrontery to borrow Lord Orpington's stallion again, but she rather thought she would not.

At just before seven o'clock she was on her way down. She no longer needed the assistance of the friendly footman who had returned to his normal duties.

As she approached the archway that led in to the cobbled yard she could see lanterns bobbing and hear voices. Unlike her previous visit, when the place had been deserted, apart from Sam and herself.

She strode through and stopped dead. Leaning nonchalantly against an open loose box door was her nemesis, Lord Orpington himself. What was he doing here so early in the morning and looking so pleased with himself?

He pushed himself away from the wall and came to meet her. He bowed, and his charming smile sent unexpected shivers through her body. 'Good morning, Mrs Sinclair. As we both prefer to ride before society is out of bed, and we both wish to ride Rufus, I thought it wise to find you another mount.' He waved in the direction of the open box from which a stamping of hoofs and jangling of harness could be heard. 'I hope that you approve of my choice.'

He turned and called to the man in

the box. 'Bring him out, Sam, before he explodes with excitement.'

Patience watched as a coal black gelding erupted from the box, Sam dangling from his bridle. With a scream of delight she raced forward to throw her arms around the animal's neck.

'Othello, my darling, where did you come from? I have missed you so.' She turned a radiant face to Simon. 'Thank you so much for bringing him down. When did he get here? Is he sufficiently rested to go out this morning?'

'Yes, he arrived two days ago. I sent for him the day you borrowed Rufus. The groom travelled post and returned in easy stages. Your side saddle arrived yesterday so you can still ride out in the afternoon without throwing the tabbies into a turmoil.'

He glanced down at the bottle green, divided riding skirt. 'That is an excellent compromise, Mrs Sinclair. Even riding astride no one could complain that you were exhibiting any more of your ankles than could be considered proper.'

Patience rewarded him with another blinding smile, deciding to forgive him, and Sam, for not telling her that her huge horse had been in residence for two whole days and she had been in ignorance of the fact.

'Shall we go? It seems an age since I last rode 'Thello. He has been with me since before my Jack was killed. He is a seasoned traveller and will have enjoyed the journey down from Ipswich.'

She turned her back and, gathering up the reins, crooked her leg for Sam to toss her in to the saddle. Even with her back turned she knew it was Orpington who gripped her boot and threw her expertly aboard her overexcited gelding.

She didn't wait to see him mounted but headed out of the other end of the stable yard, under the second archway, arriving in the gravel circle where the carriage were turned. Othello fly-kicked and sidled in his eagerness to be off. She sat, rock solid, unmoved by his performance. She had seen it all before.

'Settle down, my boy, you shall have your gallop as soon as we get to the park. It is barely a mile from here.'

Although the snow had melted the cobbles were still too slippery to risk more than a walking pace. She was fully occupied with her cavorting mount and the clatter from his hoofs made it impossible for Patience to hear if her escort was following close behind. She arrived at the park gate and urged 'Thello through, grateful she had managed to remain in the saddle and not taken a nasty tumble on the hard streets.

Finally she had time to look behind her. Relieved she could see Orpington on Rufus and Sam, on the same bay gelding he had ridden before, a short distance behind her. The soft path under foot stretched invitingly ahead. Not waiting for the others to arrive she shortened her reins, sat back in the saddle and gave her horse the office to move away.

Initially she held him to an extended

trot; she could hear the rustling of small animals in the semi-darkness and the dripping of water from black branches of the trees that lined her way. Knowing her companions were not far behind her she leant forward, squeezing her knees and Othello lengthened his stride. She held him back to a canter until he was settled then pressed again, crouching over his neck. They galloped flat-out through the deserted park scattering unsuspecting rabbits, and early morning birds, from the path.

The drumming of Othello's hoofs and the whistling of the wind past her head drowned out the sound of anything else. She had no idea how close Rufus was behind her until his huge chestnut head appeared by her knee. Laughing wildly she urged her own horse on. The two animals raced nose to nose, neither able to outpace the other. They were perfectly matched.

The path widened into a clearing allowing them both to circle their horses and bring them to a heaving halt. In the mad dash through the park Patience realised she had lost her military style hat and her hair had come free from its pins. It was tumbling in disarray around her sweat stained face. She pushed it back with one hand her eyes alight with the excitement of her ride. She had never looked so beautiful.

'That was glorious. It is not often that 'Thello meets another able to match his pace. We must arrange a true race as soon as the weather improves.'

'I would have beaten you if you had not had such a start; you were off before if I was in the park.' Simon wiped the perspiration from his face with the back of his gloved hand. 'Next time *you* ride Rufus and *I* shall take Othello. I think with less weight aboard my horse will be the winner.'

They turned as the sound of drumming hoofs alerted them that they were no longer alone. Even in the gloom they could see it was not Sam arriving so precipitously. Simon swore under his breath. Any interruption was unwelcome. He placed his horse beside hers protectively.

'Pray, excuse me, Mrs Sinclair but I believe this hat belongs to you.' The speaker, a well-built military gentlemen, smiled at Patience, his teeth a flash of white.

'Good heavens! Is that you Sir Edward? I thought you were with Nosy in Spain.' Patience edged her horse past Orpington. 'I cannot tell you how delighted I am to see you again after so long.'

She detected waves of disapproval coming from behind her and belatedly realised she should have introduced her riding companion before embarking on her greeting. She swivelled in her saddle. 'Lord Orpington, I should like to introduce you to a very dear friend of mine, Sir Edward Dalrymple. He was a mere lieutenant last time I saw him, but I can see he is a major now.'

The two men nodded, neither pleased to meet the other. Simon held out an imperious hand. 'Mrs Sinclair's hat, if you please, Major Dalrymple.'

With a grin Edward did as he was instructed. 'Are you in town for the season, Mrs Sinclair? I am staying with my married sister, Lady Davenport, in Brook Street.'

'I am visiting with my godmother, Lady Orpington. I expect to be in London until the end of the season.'

'Do I have permission to call on you?'

'Of course you do, Major Dalrymple. I shall look forward to seeing you and hearing all your news.'

The young man half-bowed and expertly turned his mount, the reins bunched up in his left hand. With a casual wave he cantered off into the distance leaving an uncomfortable silence behind him.

Patience spoke first. 'Sir Edward was a protégé of my husband's. He came to the regiment as a shy young lieutenant and I watched him grow in confidence and ability. When my husband was killed it was he who arranged his funeral and then organised my passage home. I was too distraught at the time to do more than follow his instructions. Without his help I do not think I would have survived.'

Somewhat mollified by her explanation Simon pushed Rufus closer. 'Then I owe him a debt of gratitude. He looks fit enough — I wonder why he is able to gallivant around the place whilst his regiment is fighting.'

'I believe that he has a shoulder wound. I noticed he was using only one hand on the reins. I hope he is able to remain in town for a while longer. I should dearly like to hear how the regiment progresses.'

'I think we should return. The horses are becoming chilled from standing about.'

Patience nodded, but did not answer. For some reason she could not fathom Lord Orpington had metamorphosed from charming companion to surly stranger. The sooner she was away from him the better. He was as changeable as a weathervane and she found it rather confusing. At least she knew where she was with a straightforward man like Edward Dalrymple.

* * *

Simon knew he was being unreasonable but could not help himself. Everything had been going so well. Fetching Othello from Ipswich had been a masterstroke. If Dalrymple had not appeared, decked out in his regimentals, he could have moved his plan a stage further. Patience Sinclair had issued a challenge. He was determined to make her change her mind about his eligibility as a husband. Of course he had no intention of actually marrying the wretched girl, just demonstrating to himself that he could, if he wished, offer for her and be accepted.

He had not felt so alive since his time as adjutant to the Duke of Wellington. He was no longer bored — he had a reason to get up in the morning. That his newfound enthusiasm for life was at the expense of another's feelings did not occur to him. He was so caught up in the thrill of the chase that the damage he would do to Patience if he succeeded was not even part of the equation. He saw the arrival of the major as another challenge to be surmounted. He was going to do his level best to put a spoke in that man's wheel.

* * *

Back in the privacy of her bedchamber Patience was eager to share her exciting news with her abigail and dear friend, Mary Perkins. 'Mary, you will never guess who I met on my ride. It was Edward Dalrymple. He is a major now and looked very smart in his red jacket and shako.'

'That's nice, madam. He was so kind to you after the Colonel died. Is he home on leave?'

'Lord Orpington asked the same question. I believe he thought that Sir

Edward was somehow malingering and avoiding doing his duty. I am sure that he is recovering from injury and that is why he is here and not on the Peninsula.'

'Will he be coming to see you? I expect that you would like to know how the regiment is getting on.'

'Indeed I would.' Patience tossed her hat, gloves and whip on to the bed. 'Do you know, Mary, Lord Orpington was as grumpy as a bear after Sir Edward arrived. And we had been getting on so well. When he is in a good mood he can be a charming companion.'

* * *

Mary thought it best not to enlighten her innocent young mistress as to why his lordship had been less than pleased to see Sir Edward on the scene. If downstairs gossip was correct, Mrs Sinclair had been invited to stay for the season in the hope that she would be found to be a suitable wife for the earl.

She knew that her mistress would be horrified to know she was being assessed, like a brood mare. In fact if she caught wind of this she had no doubt that they would be packed and back to Ipswich in the flick of a cat's tail.

* * *

After a refreshing bath Patience was more than ready to break her fast. Dressed in a becoming walking dress of dark gold twill, her hair freshly dressed in a neat coronet of braids, she was ready to descend.

'I should like you to accompany us to The Tower this morning, Mary. I shall be back to put on my bonnet and pelisse later.'

'Yes, ma'am. Shall Sam be coming too?'

'Of course. I feel much safer when he is with us. After so long living in the tranquillity of the countryside I find the press of people in the city overwhelming. I can hardly believe that three short years ago I was happy to follow the Colonel through thick and thin and now I am nervous just walking in the streets of London.'

Rosamond had promised to be down by 10 o'clock which meant she had an hour to eat and complete the letter she was writing to her mother. Her lips curved as she imagined the delight the news of Sir Edward's unexpected appearance would bring to her dear mama. She was still smiling as the footman opened the door to the breakfast parlour and bowed her inside.

The room was already occupied. It was a day for surprises. Lord Orpington usually took his meals in his own quarters, but here he was, relaxed and friendly, waiting by the fireplace.

'May I say how charmingly you look this morning, Mrs Sinclair? That ensemble is a perfect colour for you.'

A compliment? Whatever next? 'Thank you, sir. It is a favourite of mine. I did not look to see you here; I am used to eating on my own. Your sister and mother never come down for breakfast.'

He strolled across the room to the sideboard, groaning with silver covered-dishes full of hot food. 'Allow me to serve you, Mrs Sinclair.'

'No thank you, my lord, I much prefer to select my own. In the time it will take you to inform me as to the contents of each dish, I shall have filled my plate myself.'

Ignoring the flash of annoyance that crossed his face she smiled sunnily and began to help herself to a steaming pile of freshly scrambled eggs, a slice of ham and two hot, sweet rolls.

'I should like coffee, black if you please, my lord.' She announced as she headed for the table. A footman stepped forward and pulled out a chair for her before returning to his place by the wall.

Patience tucked in with relish. Riding always made her hungry. A few moments later she heard a second chair being moved and knew that Lord Orpington had joined her at the table.

She finished her mouthful before looking in his direction.

Her heart flipped over at the expression on his face. His dark brown eyes were glittering with something she did not recognise but the intensity of his gaze left her in no doubt that she had unwittingly annoyed her host yet again.

6

The visit to the Tower was declared a success and when Patience and Rosamond returned, it was to find Lady Orpington eagerly awaiting them in the drawing room.

'Here you are at last, my dears. I have such exciting news to share. We are to have an informal supper party on Saturday. I have received notice that several of my closest friends have now returned to London after spending Christmas and New Year in the country.'

Rosamond squealed with pleasure. 'May I wear a new gown for this event, Mama? And have you asked Beth and Amy to attend?'

'It is not the kind of party that requires one of your finest evening gowns, my dear, but certainly you may wear one of the sprigged muslins. And yes, I have invited both Beth and Amy and their mamas — as they are to come out this season I could hardly omit them from my list, now could I?'

'Is there anything I can do to help, Aunt Eleanor? After all I was invited to Orpington House in order that I help you with your planning.' Patience waited, her expression bland, but her eyes sparkling with mischief to see what answer she would get.

'Oh fiddlesticks to that! We all know why Mama invited you — it was to marry Simon.'

Lady Orpington choked on her tea. 'Whatever next! How can you say such a thing? You have put both Patience and myself to the blush. I hope you do not intend to repeat such fustian in the hearing of your brother?'

Rosamond giggled unrepentant. 'I am not run mad, Mama. I can just imagine the look on my brother's face. He would shrivel me with his fury.'

Patience noticed that her godmother's face had turned an unbecoming shade of puce. She took pity on her. 'Please do not be embarrassed, Aunt Eleanor. Both Lord Orpington and myself worked out the reason for my unexpected invitation several days ago.'

The gasps of horror that greeted her announcement made her laugh out loud.

'There is no need to look so worried; he was more amused than angry. And when I explained to him that I had no intention of marrying anyone because I enjoy being an independent woman in control of my own income and life, I am sure that he was relieved.' She smiled happily at Lady Orpington who was fanning herself furiously with a periodical.

'Indeed, Aunt Eleanor, I told him in no uncertain terms that, even if I did wish to marry, he would be the last person I should choose. I could never be happy with a directionless man — my choice would be another military gentlemen.'

'Oh my! Whatever did he say? He is

not used to being knocked back. He spends his entire time avoiding possible matrimonial traps.' Lady Orpington beamed. 'It will do him good to be put in his place for once. I am proud of you, my dear.'

'But, Mama, I thought you wished Patience and Simon to be married?'

'Lady Bryson and I merely considered the possibility. All we did was place them in the same locality, the rest was up to them. As they have taken each other in dislike, that is the end of the matter.'

The tea party disbanded at six o'clock allowing them plenty of time to change for dinner. It seemed that Lord Orpington was to grace them with his presence that evening which meant the three ladies and Miss Smithson, the colourless secretary, would be obliged to eat in the main dining room and not in the cosy, less formal small chamber they had been using.

Patience had plenty to ponder on as she sat in front of the mirror watching

Mary dress her hair. She was glad that the reason behind her visit was now in the open, but was curious to know why Orpington had suddenly decided to instigate a supper party. She smiled as she imagined his *chagrin* when Major Dalrymple arrived with the other guests. She had slipped away to visit Miss Smithson in her study and ask her to add him to the list of guests.

If they had been sitting down to a formal dinner she could not have done so without first asking Lady Orpington's permission. But as it was to be an evening of musical entertainment, charades and dancing followed by a buffet supper, an extra person could not possibly upset any seating plan. And she knew, from arranging dances for her husband at various locations, that an extra single male never came amiss.

Mary pushed in the last pin and stood back to admire her handiwork. 'There, madam, what do you think? I have left a few curls to fall around your face but restrained the rest in a knot on top of your head.'

Patience nodded. 'I love it, thank you, Mary. I was not certain about the addition of the pale green ribbons, but now I see the finished result I own that I am delighted.'

She rose gracefully to her feet and Mary bustled round shaking out the folds of the green silk dress. The décolletage was modest — revealing little, but the bodice fitted so snugly her womanly curves were clearly visible.

'I shall not be late tonight, Mary, as I wish to ride tomorrow morning if the weather is suitable. Please tell Sam.'

She was pleased that she had been able to find her two servants joint accommodation after all. They were happily established in two snug rooms on the nursery floor normally reserved for a nanny and nursemaid. This meant it was still possible to contact Mary by pulling the bell rope in the bedchamber. Of course, a kitchen maid then had to run up three flights of narrow winding stairs to pass the summons on.

However Patience had no intention of using this complicated system unless it was in an emergency.

'I shall not need you any more, Mary. Spend the evening with Sam. I can manage with Annie.'

Mary sniffed. 'That chambermaid is too flighty for my taste, madam. Thinks of nothing but footmen.'

Patience smiled. 'She is young yet, she will settle down as she gets more mature.'

'If she isn't forced to *settle down* with one of them footmen before then. But she's a helpful girl and good hearted.'

As usual there were two footmen waiting outside her rooms to light her down stairs. She was beginning to recognise some of the faces, but they all looked so similar in their white powdered half-wigs and fancy gold-frogged livery.

★　★　★

Lord Orpington was prowling up and down the drawing room resplendent in his black evening rig, a single diamond in his intricately tied stock. He paused in his pacing, his mouth curving as he remembered Mrs Sinclair's remark about him being a macaroni. He had been tempted to live up to her expectations and send his valet out to purchase him a pink and purple striped waistcoat, but he could not bring himself to do it. Instead he had made his dress even more severe than usual.

Things were not going according to his scheme. Sending for the horse had put him in a strong position, but the arrival of the heroically wounded Major Dalrymple had eclipsed his gesture. The man was the epitome of everything his quarry had stated was her preference in a mate. It was a decidedly unpleasant, and unfamiliar feeling, to know that the lady he wished to charm into compliance did not consider him an eligible parti. He had become adept over the years at making himself unpleasant to hopeful debutantes and thus depressing their hopes. Being the pursuer was a novelty.

He had no intention of seducing the delectable widow, merely engaging her affections to prove to himself that he could do so. It was a way of keeping the boredom at bay. How he wished his elder brother had not died, with his father, in the carriage accident five years ago. He had never wanted the responsibility of the title — he had wished to make a career for himself in the service of his country.

His suggestion that his mother hold an informal supper party that weekend was another move in his chess game. He would dance with Mrs Sinclair and make himself agreeable. That should be enough to soften her heart. He was not a vain man and neither was he stupid. He boxed and fenced to keep fit and could dance as well as any man in London. He saw his reflection in a glass every day and knew women found his dark good looks and athletic build irresistible. So, why was his lethal charm not working on Mrs Sinclair?

He heard the sound of feminine footsteps approaching and turned finding his heart unexpectedly accelerating with excitement. He squared his shoulders, drawing himself up to his full, impressive height.

'Mrs Sinclair, my lord.' The young footmen bowed her in and returned to his position outside the closed doors.

His mouth was unaccountably dry. What was it about the combination of magnificent emerald green eyes and dark auburn hair that he found so irresistible? No longer playing a part he smiled, his eyes glittering with appreciation.

★ ★ ★

Patience trembled and a strange sensation settled in the region of her heart. She was determined to remain immune from Orpington's charm but tonight, for the first time, she believed his devastating smile was genuine. She dipped in an elegant curtsy.

'My lord, I wish you good evening.'

This time he stepped in fast, drawing her closer as he kissed the back of her silk mittened hand. His mouth deliberately brushed the bare skin of her knuckles, where the green material ended, shooting tingles up her arm.

'You look ravisante tonight, Mrs Sinclair,' he purred.

She snatched her hand back as if it had been plunged into a fire and glared at him. What was he thinking of? She was not one of his flirts. Was he playing some sort of game with her? She recovered her composure and resisted the temptation to wipe her fingers on her gossamer wrap.

'I shall be riding tomorrow morning, my lord. Do you intend to join me?' As soon as the words had left her lips she regretted them. The last thing she wished was for him to accompany her; to give him the impression she desired his company.

He smiled again and despite her determination to remain immune she could not prevent herself responding. 'Naturally. Do you wish to ride Rufus tomorrow and have that race we spoke of the other day?'

'I should prefer to ride my own horse tomorrow, thank you. But I am happy to take up your challenge. I shall give you a head start to compensate for the weight difference, but Othello and I will still be the victors.'

'That is sporting of you, Mrs Sinclair, but unnecessary I assure you. Rufus can beat your mount without any advantages.'

They were deeply engrossed in their discussion when the other ladies finally arrived. If either of them had seen the look of satisfaction on Lady Orpington's face they would have been dismayed.

'We have kept you waiting yet again — I do apologise. I told Bentley there was no need to announce dinner, we would go straight in.'

Rosamond, decked out in another of her many white muslin gowns, ran up

to Patience. 'I love that gown, Patience.'
She peeked from under her eyelashes at
her brother. 'Do not you agree, Simon?
Does not our guest look lovely tonight?'

Simon smiled and bowed in Patience's
direction. 'Indeed she does, Rosamond,
and so I have already told her.'

He strolled across and held out his
arm, leaving Patience no choice but to
place her own on his. She found being
in such close proximity decidedly
disturbing. Wishing to disguise her lack
of composure she sailed along beside
him, back erect, a sunny smile on her
lips.

Tonight the atmosphere around the
table was gay and even his lordship
joined in the general badinage and fun.
When Lady Orpington rose Patience
was almost disappointed; she realised it
had been too long since she had
enjoyed herself. Spending an evening in
good company was quite delightful. By
the time she retired to her room she
had forgotten her reservations about
Lord Orpington. In fact she was

convinced that he was regretting his poor welcome and was now putting himself out to be charming.

* ★ ★

Simon, satisfied that he was making excellent progress with the delightful widow, decided to continue his drinking at his club. It was but a short stroll away from his house and the exercise would do him good. Warmly dressed in a top-coat, beaver on his head, cane under his arm, he was ready to step out into the night. Two burly grooms accompanied him, stout cudgel in one hand, and lantern in the other. It was not wise to venture forth unescorted. Inebriated gentlemen were easy pickings for the many footpads and pickpockets who roamed the midnight streets.

He was greeted by several of the members and invited to join in various games of cards. He refused them all — he was seeking his particular friend,

Robert, Lord Windly. He needed to talk to him about tomorrow's race. He was having second thoughts about racing a woman through the park at the crack of dawn. If word should ever leak out she would be ruined and he obliged to offer for her.

'Ah! There you are Windly. I was beginning to fear you had departed for your bed already.'

Lord Windly looked up, his broad face splitting into a grin. 'No, my friend, I was just settling in for the night. I have an excellent French brandy here — come and help me sink it.'

Two hours, and two bottles later, Simon finally remembered why he'd wished to speak to his friend. His voice was a little louder than usual and Major Dalrymple could not fail to overhear.

★   ★   ★

Mrs Sinclair was going to race her big black against Orpington's chestnut. Now that would be a race worth seeing.

He was about to drift away when the lord's next blurred words alerted him.

'I have her eating out of my hand, Windly. When I win the race tomorrow I shall demand a kiss for my prize. She will be unable to resist me and my challenge will be done.'

Dalrymple could not believe his ears. He was tempted to call the fellow out. How dare he make sport of the Colonel's widow? But then a friend appeared behind him and persuaded him to join a noisy game of chance. He had not intended to blurt out the news about the race but at some point during the card game horseflesh was spoken of.

'I tell you what, you won't find a better matched pair than Orpington's chestnut and Mrs Sinclair's black.' Before he knew it word was spreading around the club and wagers of thousands of pounds were being entered in the book. It was a disaster. He had to warn them — tell them not to race as half of the *ton* was intending to come to watch.

He tottered home to his apartments with every intention of rising at dawn and rushing to Orpington House but it was after eight when he finally roused from his drunken stupor. He flung on his clothes and ran out — maybe Orpington had overslept and he would still be in time. If the race went ahead Mrs Sinclair would be ruined and Orpington would not fare much better.

7

Patience had no worries about any possible danger to her reputation or her person posed by the race. She knew that at dawn there would be nobody around to see. She was dressed and on her way to the stable before the clock stuck seven.

Orpington was there before her, his expression serious. 'Good morning, Mrs Sinclair. I am having considerable misgivings about this event. I think it might be best if we forgot all about it and made this a normal early morning ride.'

'Are you running scared, my lord? I had not thought you weak-spirited. I wish to go ahead — but of course cannot do so on my own.'

She had said exactly the right thing to provoke him into agreement. 'If that is your wish then so be it. Shall we say three miles? The distance from the entrance of the park to the circle is a mile and a half — there and back should do it.'

'Excellent. What about a prize?'

He smiled. 'I thought the loser should grant a boon of the winner's choosing. Are you agreeable?'

This seemed innocuous enough. 'Yes — that is acceptable.'

They clattered out of the yard, closely followed by Sam and a groom. Othello, having been unexercised for several days, was jumping out of his skin with excitement Patience was so occupied with remaining in the saddle that she failed to notice the unusual amount of male pedestrians in the vicinity of the park.

She was having difficulty holding her horse back. 'Shall we go as soon as we reach the path? I doubt 'Thello will stand for a formal start.'

'Agreed. Let me come along side you now so that we can enter the gate at the same time.' Lord Orpington edged

Rufus closer but he lashed out, his yellow teeth almost removing a chunk from Othello's neck. 'Damnation! You must go ahead, Mrs Sinclair. I cannot risk an accident.'

Patience was determined to have no unfair advantage and managed to hold her mount back long enough for Rufus to draw alongside. As soon as he was level she flung herself forward and kicked her horse hard. They shot off and were soon several lengths ahead.

The wind whistled through her hair as she crouched over 'Thello's withers urging him faster. They were in a flat gallop; she bent low over his neck and for an awful second thought she saw a row of gawping faces standing by the side of the path. No — she was mistaken — it was the evergreen shrubs deceiving her.

They reached the large grass circle at the end of the path and Patience pulled hard on the inside rein pressing her right calf into her horse's side to indicate that he was to turn. He responded by shortening his stride to an extended canter. As he swung, he executed a flying change of legs before returning to a gallop.

This time she was not mistaken. The roaring cheer that greeted her horsemanship echoed round the space. All she saw were flashes of white as she thundered past, but it was enough to realise that her private wager with Lord Orpington had somehow become common knowledge. The park was full of gentlemen of various ages, all come out expressly to witness her total disgrace.

She was sure that her opponent had seen the watchers and would be equally horrified. His good name was at risk too. Distracted she stopped concentrating on her mount and he began to slow allowing the chestnut to overtake. As the horse sped past she caught a fleeting glimpse of Orpington's face — he was laughing. How could he laugh? Was it possible he had not noticed the lookers-on because of his determination to win the race?

The outcome was irrelevant now — whatever happened she was the loser. Her reputation was in tatters — she would be obliged to return to Bryson Court immediately. The exit to the park was approaching — she should be reining back but impulsively she urged her black horse on, scattering the crowd of cheering, hat-waving gentlemen in all directions.

She narrowly missed impaling herself on the park railings as Othello hurtled out into the road his metal shod hooves skidding on the wet cobbles. She barely managed to remain in the saddle struggling to right herself, her foot now swinging out of the stirrup, adding to her lack of balance.

She could not fall. She would not fall. Landing on the cobbles at the speed they were travelling could prove fatal. She could hear shouts behinds her but ignored them. Somehow she scrambled straight and jammed her boot home in the swinging iron. Othello sensing her danger had slowed down, allowing her the time she needed to adjust her seat and regain control.

The sounds of voices had faded into the distance. She was alone in the street. It was safe to reduce her speed. She sat back in the saddle and flexed her fingers; her horse immediately dropped down to a collected canter, to a trot and finally to a walk. Patience looked around checking she had not become lost in her mad flight from the park. No — thank goodness — she was almost at the turning into Grosvenor Square.

She met no-one else and clattered back into the yard desperate to dismount and get inside before Orpington arrived. She did not need him to lecture her on her immodest behaviour. She was well aware just how stupid she had been. What was acceptable in Spain where convention was ignored was totally beyond the pale in London. She would have a bath and change into her travelling clothes. It would not take Mary and Sam long to pack both her trunks and their own. She would send Harry, the friendly footman, to book her a place on the midday mail coach. She could be on her way home before the scandal broke over the house.

Then she remembered that someone would have to return her beloved black. Sam couldn't do it — it was essential that he escort them on the coach. Without a male escort one left oneself open to insult and unpleasantness from other passengers. Well, Orpington had been responsible for fetching him from her home so he would just have to arrange for his return.

At her unaccompanied arrival the lone stable boy, idling his time away sitting on an upturned bucket, leapt to his feet sending it rolling noisily across the cobbles. The unexpected arrival of the pail caused Othello to rear up throwing his rider backwards against the brickwork of the archway.

Patience cried out once as her head smashed into the wall then she tumbled unconscious from the saddle. The animal crashed down, narrowly missing the inert body spread-eagled on the ground. The pandemonium brought men running and whilst one caught the flying reins another dropped to his knees beside the injured girl.

★ ★ ★

It was only as Simon thundered past the black stallion that he realised why he had been able to overtake. He finally saw what Patience had seen earlier — their private race had become spectacularly public. His triumph vanished to be replaced by furious rage. Someone had revealed his business and woe betide the man who had done it when *he* got hold of him.

His mind raced as fast as his horse as he tried to think of a way to save the situation — save Mrs Sinclair's reputation. His expression grim he heaved on the reins and prepared to bring his mount to a standstill. He had no choice. He must introduce her as his fiancé, for only then could society accept her outrageous behaviour without censure. With a wry smile he sat back, so his Mama's little scheme had worked after all. Finally she would have her dearest wish — a daughter-in-law. He was well and truly caught in parson's mousetrap so why was he feeling a growing sense of joy and not the sense of dread one would expect?

Could it be possible that after so long he had fallen in love? Had found a woman he wished to spend the rest of his life with? He had no time to mull these thoughts over as, to his astonishment, the lady of his dreams galloped straight past him and towards the wrought iron gate. His heart flew into his mouth as her horse almost lost his footing and shot her off onto the railings. Would she right herself or would he find her fatally injured in the street outside?

He kicked Rufus from a halt to a gallop, ignoring the men flocking towards him, and followed his intended through the gates of the park. He reached the exit to find the road ahead clear — no bodies, no horse. His breath hissed from between clenched teeth. She was safe, but for how long? If she continued home at that pace she would surely meet with an accident.

Leaving his groom and her man Perkins to follow as they would, he urged his horse into a canter. He rounded every corner expecting to see disaster and each time Patience was not there he said a prayer of gratitude. Not given to speaking to the almighty, apart from his Sunday visits to church, he hoped his words would somehow find their way.

He turned into Grosvenor Square and the road was clear. He pulled his mount back to a trot — no need to hurry, she was safely home. Feeling relaxed and happier than he'd ever felt in his life, he rode through the gravel turning circle to find his worst nightmare realised. Stretched out, deathly pale, a growing pool of dark, viscous blood pooling under her head, was the woman he loved more than life itself.

Vaulting from the saddle and throwing his reins to a waiting groom, he joined the man on his knees beside the unconscious form.

'Jethro, has the physician been sent for? Has word been sent to the house?'

His voice cracked with the whip of authority across the group of men temporarily paralysed by the horror of the accident. Immediately order was restored from chaos.

The head groom called over to the young man holding the reins of the chestnut. 'Ned, take his lordship's horse and get round fast to Doctor Jenkins. You know his direction, lad, you went there to fetch him when young Peter broke his arm last winter.' Jethro turned to the stable lad clinging for dear life to an agitated Othello. 'Jim, give the gelding to me, and run up to the house and alert them.'

Simon, meanwhile, was ripping off

his neck cloth and folding it into a pad. Head wounds bled like the very devil; he prayed that was the reason there was so much gore. Gently he lifted her head from the cobbles and placed his makeshift bandage over the injury. Pressing hard with his right hand whilst he scooped her up onto his lap.

'Jethro, I need your assistance.' When the man was down beside him he told him what he wanted. 'Here, put your hand on the pad and keep it hard against her head. Is that clear?'

The man nodded. 'Yes, my lord.'

'Good man. I am going to stand up and take Mrs Sinclair inside. Are you ready?'

Simon straightened his legs, throwing his weight back as he lifted. He had no intention of dropping his precious bundle. The groom managed his task well and together the two men made slow progress towards the side entrance.

As they arrived the door flew back to reveal Lady Rosamond. 'Simon, what has happened? The groom said there had been an accident in the stable.'

'Out of the way, Rosamond. I must get Mrs Sinclair into the warm. Her habit is soaked through where she fell onto the cobbles.'

The distraught girl stepped to one side allowing her brother to stride by. He knew it would be fruitless to ask his sister to assist; she fainted at the sight of blood. Mary Perkins, the abigail, would know how to deal with this emergency. She appeared to be a resourceful woman and had travelled all over the continent with her mistress.

He took the stairs cautiously; his assistant had to keep pace. They arrived outside Mrs Sinclair's apartment to be greeted by Mary, pale but ready to do whatever was necessary to help.

'Bring her right through into the bed-chamber, my lord, if you please.'

The two men followed her into the inner sanctum and Simon was relieved to see two chamber maids ready to assist. The fire was roaring and the room warm. As he placed the comatose girl on the bed, he transferred his own hand to the red-soaked pad. Jethro, embarrassed to be in such a fine chamber in his boots sloped off through the servant's door kindly pointed out to him by one of the girls.

'Mrs Sinclair has a serious head injury. She has already lost a deal of blood. It is essential that pressure is kept on the wound until the surgeon arrives to stitch it up.'

'You can leave Mrs Sinclair in my care, my lord. I have nursed far worse than this.'

He watched her hand a folded pad of white cotton to one of the girls.

'Jen, when his lordship removes his hand you place the pad over the one there. Don't let it fall away. Is that clear?

'Yes, Mrs Perkins.'

The transfer was successfully completed and Simon was able to step back. 'I shall leave her in your capable hands, Mrs Perkins. I shall be outside in the sitting room. I wish to be here when the doctor arrives.'

'Very well, my lord. We shall get Mrs Sinclair warm and dry in a trice.'

He took a last look at the ashen faced woman and his heart twisted with fear. He knew from bitter experience that the longer a patient remained unconscious the more gloomy the prognosis. His brother, Charles, had received just such a head injury and remained as if dead for weeks. Long enough for him to return and say his farewells before Charles finally gave up the ghost and joined their father in heaven. Two Lord Orpingtons buried in as many months.

He paced the carpet unaware that his boots were leaving muddy trails behind him. Where was the damn doctor? He only lived a few streets away — he should be here by now. He heard footsteps outside and turned expectantly.

'Enter,' he called before the knock was finished. The door opened and not

Dr Jenkins but the elderly butler, Bentley, stood there a silver salver on his upturned, white gloved, palm.

'I am sorry to disturb you, my lord, but there is a Sir Edward Dalrymple downstairs who wishes to speak urgently with you.'

'Tell him to go to the devil! Where is the doctor, Bentley? That is the man I wish to see.'

'I shall send Doctor Jenkins up as soon as he arrives, my lord. I shall ask Sir Edward to wait in the small drawing room until you are free.'

Simon wanted to throw a missile at the man. How could he be so unmoved when his beloved Patience was at death's dark door? He sank on to a *chaise-longue* dropping his head into his hands to pray. His prayers had fallen on deaf ears so far — could it be that God ignored those who had done the same to him? He vowed that he would do more than pay lip-service to his maker if, *when*, Patience was restored to him.

Doctor Jenkins found him like this when he arrived ten minutes later. 'My lord, I am sorry to intrude in your moment of prayer.'

Simon shot up. 'Thank God you are come. Go in, man, go in. They are expecting you.' He watched the short, middle-aged man disappear and he heard the murmur of voices behind the closed door. How much longer must he stand in agony waiting to hear how things were?

8

A slight noise alerted him that the doctor was emerging from the sick room. Simon scanned his face searching for clues. 'Well, sir? How is Mrs Sinclair?'

The doctor bowed. 'I am relieved to tell you, my lord, that Mrs Sinclair is suffering from a slight concussion. The head wound, which I have sutured, will be uncomfortable for a day or so, but is in no immediate danger.'

'Thank God for that! I had feared the situation was far worse. Has she regained consciousness?'

'Briefly, but she is sleeping now. If she does not develop a morbid fever she will make a full recovery. Mrs Sinclair is a healthy young woman and her maid assures me she has suffered far worse in the past and been up and riding within days of the injury.'

'Thank you, Doctor Jenkins. You will be calling again later, I presume?' Simon's tone made it clear this was not a request.

'I shall be back to check on my patient this evening, my lord. But please do not hesitate to send for me earlier if you have any concerns.'

The doctor was escorted from the bedchamber by a waiting footman. Simon debated whether to wait where he was until Mrs Sinclair was well enough to see him or return to the library.

He frowned, recalling that Bentley had said Dalrymple was waiting to speak to him. He sincerely hoped the young man would have had the sense to take his leave by now.

The entrance hall was silent. He guessed his mother and sister were waiting in the small drawing room to hear the doctor's prognosis. He strode across and as he paused, waiting for a servant to open the door, he detected the sound of an unfamiliar male voice conversing with his mother and sister.

Cursing under his breath he barged past the footman and walked straight in. Three heads turned as one. Dalrymple jumped to his feet, his face pale. His expression unfriendly.

'My Lord, how is Mrs Sinclair? I could not depart without having first ascertained she was in no danger from her accident.'

Simon did not return his bow. 'I had not thought to find you here, Dalrymple. This is a matter for family.'

The two men eyed each other; the dislike and contempt on the face of the soldier made Simon wonder what he had done to offend him. He could sense the embarrassment of the ladies at such overt hostility and knew it was his role to defuse the scene.

Ignoring the major he turned to his mother. 'Mama, I am delighted to be able to tell you that Mrs Sinclair has suffered no lasting harm from her fall. She has gashed her head and has a mild concussion. Doctor Jenkins is sanguine that she will make a full recovery. He is returning to check on her this evening.'

'Thank the Lord. I have sent cards to everybody cancelling the party for tomorrow night. I shall rearrange it as soon as Patience is fully recovered.' Lady Orpington patted Rosamond's hand. 'There, you see, my dear; I told you there was nothing to worry about.'

Satisfied he had reassured his relatives Simon turned his attention to the unwanted visitor.

Icily correct he bowed in his direction. 'Sir Edward, I believe you wish to speak to me. Shall we repair to the library and leave the ladies to their embroidery?' He turned on his heel, allowing the younger man no choice, and stalked from the room.

The library door was open and Simon walked straight in to stop, his back pointedly to the door, in front of the cheery fire. He sensed that the soldier was behind him. He waited several minutes before turning.

'Well, you are *de trop*, Dalrymple.

Speak your piece. I have more important things to do.' He watched the man flush and saw his fists clench, realising, too late, that he had possibly misjudged the situation.

'Orpington, I must tell you that I overheard you talking about the race. I was in my cups and inadvertently revealed what I had heard. Before I realised, wagers were being placed in the book and plans being made to come and watch the event. I intended to come at dawn to advise you to cancel but did not wake in time. I am deeply ashamed of my part in Mrs Sinclair's accident.'

Simon understood that he was equally to blame. In fact, entirely to blame. He relaxed and smiled. 'You have no need to apologise, Sir Edward, I should not have been discussing the event in public. The blame is all mine. And have no fear I intend to put matters right. Mrs Sinclair shall suffer no damage to her reputation. You may be the first to wish me happy. We are to be married.'

For some reason this news did nothing to remove the look of dislike from the young man's face. There was more to this than he had first thought. Was Dalrymple infatuated? Had he hoped to secure Patience for himself? Indeed, he was exactly the kind of man she had professed to prefer. Had he finally found the woman he could share the rest of his life with, only to lose her to another?

★　★　★

Never! His eyes narrowed and he glared across the room, daring the major to comment adversely on his announcement. To his astonishment Dalrymple merely nodded his head and turned, to march briskly from the room. Simon shook his head. What did this extraordinary behaviour indicate? Was Dalrymple a rival or not?

He walked over to the desk and slumped disconsolately into the leather chair beside it. He had known Patience

Sinclair for scarcely more than a se'ennight and he had fallen, neck over crop, in love with her. He had scoffed, often enough, at the antics of his peers when they had professed themselves smitten. Now he understood what made them behave in such a way. He realised that he would do anything, say anything, to secure his darling's agreement.

* * *

Patience tried to raise her head but a wave of nausea overcame her and she flopped back weakly on the pillows. Her head hurt abominably. Cautiously she raised a trembling hand to touch the bandage that encircled her forehead. What had happened? How had she come to be injured and lying in her bed with the curtains drawn?

'Madam, you're awake. You took a nasty tumble in the stable yard and have a slight concussion and a nasty gash on the back of your head. The doctor has stitched you up and says you will be back on your feet in a day or two.' Mary smoothed the rumpled covers as she spoke.

Patience frowned and wished that she had not. The gesture caused a sharp stab pain in the back of her head. 'How did I fall? I never come off.'

'Your horse was startled by a rolling pail and reared up. Unfortunately you were passing under the archway at the time and your head hit the bricks and you were knocked unconscious.'

'Yes, I do vaguely remember it now. Poor 'Thello, he will be distraught. How did I get here?'

'Lord Orpington carried you up, madam, as if you were no more than a feather in his arms.'

'Where is he now? I hope he is not lurking outside in my parlour. I have no wish to speak to him. Do not on any account allow him entry, is that clear, Mary?'

Puzzled, her maid nodded. 'Yes, ma'am. Her ladyship has sent up to enquire as to how you are doing and there is a basket of fruit and an enormous bouquet of hothouse flowers in your parlour.'

'Did the physician indicate when I should be well enough to travel?'

'No, he didn't. But I should think by Monday you will be up and about.'

'In that case make sure that my trunks are packed and ready on that day. I shall ask Lady Orpington if she will allow me to borrow her travelling carriage because I intend to return home. My reputation has gone. My disgraceful behaviour will be the talk of the *ton*. I cannot allow my disgrace to spoil Lady Rosamond's debut.'

'I understand, madam. I'm sure that things are not as bad as you imagine. But you will do better recuperating in the peace the countryside.'

★　★　★

Three days after her accident Patience was ready to depart. She had steadfastly refused to speak to Lord Orpington but had explained the situation to his mother and she appeared to understand and supported her in her desire for solitude.

The return journey to Bryson Court was quite different from the journey to London two weeks previously. This time she travelled in luxury, two outriders in attendance and luxurious accommodation arranged at Romford and Colchester. Sam rode alongside on Othello. The decision to break the journey twice had been taken without her consent. Patience was too dispirited to question any of the arrangements.

As they approached the Dower House at lunchtime on the third day, she tried unsuccesfully to be glad she was home. Her heart was heavy; she had left her mother full of eager anticipation, expecting to enjoy several months of balls and parties and here she was returning in disgrace hardly more than two weeks later. Lady Orpington had offered no objection when she had asked to borrow the carriage. She had half hoped she would be persuaded by her hostess to change her mind, but this had not been the case. Her godmother had agreed with everything she said.

Indeed, she had been given the distinct impression that the sooner she left, the happier everyone would be. Even dear Rosamond had appeared embarrassed in her company. Patience shifted uncomfortably on the squabs. No, not embarrassed exactly, more secretive — as though she was bursting with information that she was not allowed to divulge.

She sighed. It was useless speculating, for she was now home. It was unlikely she would be invited to visit again. She was *persona non grata* in London. If only dear Jack was still alive and she was still in the warmth and excitement of the Peninsular, an integral part of the regiment, her life filled with excitement and purpose.

Her eyes filled with tears. Angrily she

brushed them aside. It was too late to repine. She had to get on with her life as it was. Make the most of the things that she had. Why did being an independent woman no longer seem important? Why could she not shake off the image of the dark eyed, dark haired, perfidious Lord Orpington from her head?

She had a letter for her mother from Aunt Eleanor. Hopefully this would mean she did not have to relive every embarrassing detail of her debacle. The sooner she forgot everyone in London the quicker she would recover her spirits.

Her arrival at the Dower House was expected and after a fond embrace from her mother, she was bustled upstairs and into bed. Lady Orpington had sent a letter so everything was prepared. She wanted to protest that she was not an invalid, that she had no wish to retire but somehow lethargy and low spirits prevented her and she was glad to sink back into the privacy of her curtained bed. She remembered the letter for her mother still in her reticule.

'Mary, please give Lady Bryson the letter from Lady Orpington. It is in my bag. I shall not need you any more today. Come to me, as usual, at eight o'clock tomorrow morning.'

Patience heard the door close softly behind Mary and closed her eyes. Her sutures pulled painfully in her scalp and meant that she could not rest on her back but was obliged to curl either on her left or right. She was surprised that her mother was not at her side fussing. Sadly she realised that her behaviour had been so shocking that even her devoted parent was disgusted with her. She shuddered to think what her strait-laced brother had made of the matter.

She dozed fitfully all afternoon. It was the rumbling of her stomach that finally forced her out of bed. She pulled the bell strap and waited for the chambermaid to appear in answer to her summons. To her surprise it was not the servant's door that opened it was the door that led to her parlour.

'Darling girl, are you feeling more the thing? I thought we could have tea together in your parlour. Let me help you put on your wrap.'

Patience held out her arms and allowed her mother to dress her. Had she been mistaken? This was not the behaviour of an outraged parent. 'I am so sorry, Mama . . . '

'Enough. You shall not apologise for something that was not your fault. Come, my dear, take my arm and I shall help you to the table.'

In the pretty, well furnished sitting-room an apple-wood fire burnt merrily in the grate. Patience saw a substantial high tea had been laid out on the table and two chairs placed conveniently beside it. She was surprised to discover that they were to serve themselves.

'Here, my dear girl, you take the seat nearest the fire. I thought we should like to be private so I shall pour the tea.'

There was no attempt to make

conversation until they had both eaten their fill. Patience pushed away her crumb-filled plate. 'That was delicious, Mama. Thank you. I do not believe that I have eaten a proper meal since my accident. Cook has surpassed herself.'

'I am so glad that you were able to do it justice. Now, my dear, do you feel well enough to talk?'

Patience nodded. 'I had thought that I was in disgrace. I should never have suggested racing Lord Orpington.'

'His lordship should never have accepted. The blame is entirely his. He knows how things are in society; you do not. But he is devastated by what happened to you and is intending to come down and apologise in person as soon as you are fully recovered.'

Patience felt sick. 'No, he must not. I do not wish to see him. He betrayed me to his friends and he laughed when he saw them there. His sole objective was to send me home. He saw me as a threat to his bachelor state.'

Her mother looked at her as if she

had recently escaped from Bedlam. 'Do not be so ridiculous, Patience. It was not he who revealed your plans, but another. He was overheard discussing the race with his best friend. The matter would have gone no further if the man who had overheard had not spread the word.'

'I see.' But she did not. Her emotions were in turmoil; it had been so much easier to blame Orpington. Cordially disliking him for his behaviour meant that she did not have to think about the way his smile made her feel weak and his slightest touch sent her pulse racing.

'When is he coming, Mama?' Perhaps she could make sure she was visiting her aunt in Bath at the time.

'I am to send word when you are ready to receive visitors. I expect you would prefer to have your stitches removed first so that you can dress your hair. Mary tells me they will be ready to come out tomorrow or the next day. Therefore I shall pen a note to Eleanor inviting Lord Orpington to visit. I expect we can anticipate his arriving at the weekend.'

Fixing a false smile to her trembling lips Patience answered. 'It is quite unnecessary for him to journey so far in order to apologise. A letter would suffice.'

Why was her mother looking so pleased? Was she so starved of company that the visit of a comparative stranger filled her with excitement?

'He insists on coming in person, my dear. He feels personally responsible for the curtailment of your visit. I believe he is hoping to persuade you to return when you are recovered.'

Patient shuddered. 'No, I shall not go back to London. I think I should like to spend some time with Aunt Elizabeth in Bath. It is less hectic there, but equally convivial. Shall you come with me? It is almost a year since Aunt Elizabeth visited here.'

'If that is what you wish, my dear, I shall be happy to accompany you. As long as you are prepared to go back into society, it matters not to me if it is in Bath or London.'

A letter had been sent to London and also to Lady Fitzwilliam in Bath. Plans were made to put the house under Holland covers and their departure date was set for the day after Lord Orpington's visit, whenever that might be.

Patience had just returned from her early-morning ride and was on her way upstairs when she caught sight of a horseman cantering down the drive. His caped riding coat and tricorn hat obscured his face. Her heart leapt into her throat. Did she have time to change before her visitor arrived? Orpington must have set out the moment her mother's letter had arrived.

Something bright caught her eye. She ran lightly back down the stairs to stand in front of one off the windows that flanked the front door. Surely she was mistaken? No, she was correct. This was not Lord Orpington arriving it was Sir Edward Dalrymple. Why on earth was he coming here?

9

Patience decided she would not receive the unexpected visitor in her mired riding habit. She hurried from the hall ringing the small brass bell as she passed it.

'Yes, Mrs Sinclair, how can I help?' The housekeeper smiled waiting for her instructions. The Dower House was an all-female establishment and consequently had no footmen or butler.

'There is a gentleman, Sir Edward Dalrymple, about to arrive at our front door. Please show him into the drawing room and inform him that I shall join him in a very short while. Also, ask Cook to prepare some refreshments. Sir Edward will have ridden a long way this morning.'

If the housekeeper thought that her decision to entertain a gentleman without her mother as chaperone unladylike, Patience was glad she kept the thought to herself. Upstairs Mary had prepared her bath as usual.

'I do not have time for a long soak, this morning, Mary. Sir Edward is about to arrive downstairs. I must bathe quickly for I am eager to see him and discover why he has felt the need to venture so far to see me.'

'Would you like me to come down with you, madam? Seeing as Lady Bryson is at The Court and not available.'

'That will not be necessary, thank you, Mary. I have known Sir Edward for many years. What is left of my reputation is in no danger from a visit with him.'

Fashionably dressed in a long sleeved, dark gold promenade-dress, a Kashmir shawl around her shoulders and a dainty white lace cap on her head to cover her injury, Patience was ready to descend less than twenty minutes later.

She paused outside the drawing room to collect herself; it would not do to appear flustered in any way. Leaving the door open, thus satisfying the proprieties, she walked gracefully in to join Sir Edward. He was standing with his back to the door staring pensively into the fire. She was struck afresh by his impressive stature, by the width of his shoulders, emphasised by the snug fit of his scarlet regimental jacket.

'Sir Edward, welcome. It is delightful to see you so far from London.'

He turned on his heel and bowed correctly. 'I must apologise for disturbing you in your home, Mrs Sinclair, but there are things that I must say to you that I could not put in to a letter.'

Patience felt as if she had swallowed a stone. He was going to propose marriage to her. She did not wish to marry him, even if it meant she could return to the regiment. She dipped her head to hide her expression and settled herself on a plain, bentwood chair.

'Please be seated, Sir Edward. I have arranged for refreshments to be brought. I am sure you must be sharp set after your long ride.'

He nodded and folded his long legs on to a matching chair at a respectable distance from her own. 'I have come from Colchester, I am stationed there at present. I am to return to Spain with a contingent of new recruits at the end of the month.'

There was an awkward pause; the only sound the crackling of the logs in the grate. He cleared his throat. Patience braced herself. She prayed he would not go down on one knee; it would be so difficult to refuse him if he was kneeling before her.

'I have come here to apologise to you. I have already done so to Lord Orpington. The fact that your race became public knowledge was entirely down to me. I overheard Orpington discussing it and mentioned it to a crony. Before I knew, word had travelled round the club.'

Thank God! He had not come to propose but to apologise. She smiled at him. 'There is no need to say any more, Orpington was to blame. If he had not been so indiscreet you would not have known about the event.'

He grinned sheepishly. 'That may be true, but I should not have repeated something I heard in a private conversation. If I had not been bosky, I should not have done so. Also I had intended to rise at dawn in order to ride over to Orpington House and warn you not to race. I overslept.'

'Let us say no more about it.'

Their conversation became more general. Patience was eager to know everything about Dalrymple's new posting. When a parlour maid brought in the expected refreshments, they were relaxed and comfortable in each other's company.

She picked at the food but the major fell to with gusto. Whilst he ate, she sipped her coffee mulling over what he had told her. If she was prepared to excuse Sir Edward for his indiscretion then she must do the same for Orpington. She felt her heart slowly thawing and it was as if a black cloak of misery had been lifted from her shoulders.

He was coming to see her in a day or two. She felt herself tingling with anticipation and her happiness was reflected on her face. 'Major Dalrymple, it was so kind of you to take the time to explain in person. Lord Orpington is expected here as well.'

The young man nodded believing he understood the reason for her happiness. 'I am glad that you have found it in your heart to forgive him. Not many ladies would be so generous.'

'He had consumed a prodigious amount of claret that evening, like you, sir, he spoke without thought. I am sure it was not his intention for his words to be passed round the club.'

'I am glad that you can put the matter of his challenge behind you. Matters were obviously different when he made it.'

She frowned. What was he talking about? She knew of no challenge. Should she admit her ignorance or pretend she understood and hope her guest would reveal more? She decided to follow the latter procedure.

'Naturally I was shocked, but in the circumstances I decided to forgive him that as well.' She hoped her words did not make as little sense to him as they did to her.

'You are a generous lady. I hope when I fall in love, it will be with someone as forgiving as yourself.' He smiled, replacing his plate and cutlery on the side table. 'But then I hope I would never do anything so ungallant as to wager with my friends that I could win the lady's affections.'

Patience stared at him not believing she had heard him correctly. She leapt to her feet, in her agitation forgetting she was supposed to know all about this challenge. 'Are you telling me that Orpington was trifling with my affections? His attentions were merely to win his wager?'

The major scrambled to his feet. 'I know that he was not doing so, Mrs

Sinclair. For he told me the day of your accident that you were betrothed.'

She felt her coffee flooding back into her mouth and knew she had to leave the room before she disgraced herself by casting up her accounts on the poor man's boots. With her hand to her mouth she fled upstairs reaching her dressing room just in time.

As she retched helplessly, Mary rubbed her back, holding her braid away from her face. Eventually her stomach was empty and Patience stepped back from the noxious mess. She had ice flowing through her veins not blood.

'Mary, please go downstairs and ask Sir Edward to take his leave. Tell him I am unwell. Then send the stable boy up to the Court and ask Lady Bryson to return at once.' She paused, surprised her voice sounded so natural when her heart was in pieces. 'Ask Sam to get the travelling carriage ready. We shall leave for Bath immediately.'

She was glad that Mary did not

question her commands. She did not think she could bear to give the reasons why. Not yet. The hurt was too raw. In the space of an hour she had ascended to the heights of happiness only to crash back even further into the depths of desolation. She had been betrayed, made a mockery of. Orpington was not offering to marry her out of love, but out of duty.

She collapsed on the bed fighting back the tears. She was determined not to weep for the loss of her dream. She was an independent woman and would remain that way. Nothing had changed. Two weeks ago she had told Orpington he was the last man she would choose to marry. She had not changed her opinion.

Scrubbing her eyes with her sleeve she rolled upright. She had work to do if they were to leave in the next hour. Luckily the trunks were already packed; it should not take long to place them in the baggage coach and send them on their way. Aunt Elizabeth was expecting them, what would it matter if they arrived a few days earlier than arranged?

Orpington could already be on his way. She was determined not to see him. She knew his silver tongue and charming smile might persuade her to accept him and make her believe that she had no choice. If she was not there for him to ask then she would be safe. She could not marry him feeling the way she did. An unrequited love was the worst possible basis for a relationship.

Lady Bryson listened quietly to the garbled explanation. 'The man is a monster. I truly thought his affections were engaged. Eleanor said so in her letter. She was cock-a-hoop, believing that her son had finally fallen in love and was ready to get married. She will be devastated to discover his duplicity.' She embraced her daughter fondly. 'I shall pen a note to your brother and then I shall be ready to leave. Do not worry, my dear, we shall be away from here before that rogue arrives.'

'We shall not have bespoken accommodation. I thought we could send Sam ahead, on Othello, to organise that for us. If he leaves immediately he will make better time and can arrange rooms at The Lion, in Colchester.'

'That is an excellent idea, Patience. Is the matter in hand?'

'It is, Mama. Mary has to remove my sutures before we leave. She is in the kitchen boiling up some water and the scissors. I wish to be able to put my hair up and wear a bonnet. I do not wish to draw attention to myself on the journey.'

'Very well, that will allow me time to oversee the packing for the journey and to change into my travelling gown. It is fortuitous that the weather is cold for that should make travelling easier. Five days in a coach when the roads are wet and muddy does not bear thinking of.'

All was bustle and busyness for the next hour as the housekeeper supervised the loading of the trunks into the smaller coach and Cook prepared a hamper for the journey. Sam departed with strict instructions not to tire his mount, but still to arrive in time to reserve rooms for the night.

At 11 o'clock the Dower House was under holland covers, the baggage coach had left containing two maids and the trunks, and Lord Bryson's carriage was standing outside on the gravel, the four matching bay geldings stamping and eager to depart.

'Come along, Mama, we must not keep the horses waiting. It is too cold.' Patience led the way, but stood aside to allow her mother to ascend the steps into the carriage. Mary placed a hot brick at her mother's feet and a rug over her knees.

'Are you ready, Mama?' Patience asked, eager to get going.

'I am. Tell Tom Coachman to depart. It will be dark in a few hours and I do not enjoy travelling at night, especially in the winter.'

Patience banged on the roof with the carved bone handle of her riding whip and the carriage rumbled forward. She did not breathe easily until they were safely on the main coaching road that linked Ipswich to Colchester.

* * *

It was dusk when Lord Orpington galloped down the drive to the Dower House. He was riding Rufus, but his luxurious travelling carriage was following behind. He had every expectation that Patience would be returning with him to London.

He reined back in a flurry of gravel. The house was in darkness, the shutters across, no flicker of light anywhere. Vaulting from the saddle he looped his reins over his arm and strode to the door. He raised the knocker and hammered. He had a bad feeling about this; something was wrong.

10

Lord Orpington heard footsteps approaching the door. Good, there was someone in residence after all. He heard the sound of bolts and keys being pulled and turned and watched the door swing back.

'I am sorry to keep you waiting, sir, but as you can see Lady Bryson and Mrs Sinclair are visiting elsewhere. You will find Lord Bryson at the big house.'

Before he could reply the woman closed the door firmly leaving him no choice. Bryson Court was now his destination. Why had Patience gone away when she knew he was coming to see her? He had a sinking feeling that he was not going to like the answer to this question.

He rammed his foot home in the stirrup iron and swung back into the saddle. 'Come, Rufus, let us go up to speak to Lord Bryson. I promise that you shall be able to rest once I have solved this mystery.'

Simon cantered up the gently curving drive and reined in at the foot of the imposing white marble staircase that led up to a portico, which had three massive columns supporting it on either side. It was of recent construction and he realised he was not arriving at the abode of a country squire. Lord Bryson was a wealthy man with excellent taste.

Before he could dismount a stable boy appeared at his side and grasped Rufus by the bit.

'Good morning, my lord, we was expecting you this afternoon. You 'ave made good time from Colchester.'

Curiouser and curiouser! Handing his reins to the boy he strode up the steps fully expecting the massive front door to open before he reached it. He was not disappointed. The butler bowed deeply.

'Welcome, Lord Orpington. Lord Bryson is expecting you. Will your luggage be arriving shortly?'

'It will. My man is travelling behind me with my necessities. He should be here in an hour or so.' He followed the august gentleman into Bryson Court and looked around with interest at the vast expanse of chequered floor from which various doors and passageways led. He observed a central staircase ascending to an impressive upper hallway.

'If you would care to refresh yourself before joining his lordship in the study, the housekeeper, Mrs Johnson shall show you to your room.'

Simon glanced down; his boots were mud spattered, his britches and topcoat in no better state. He nodded to the tall, spare woman, also dressed in black.

'Please come with me, Lord Orpington.' The lady led the way up the massive staircase and along the wide carpeted hallway stopping halfway along. The footman who had accompanied them opened the door and bowed him in.

The chamber was a private sitting-room, well appointed with an *escritoire*, several comfortable armchairs, a variety of marquetry tables and a floor-to-ceiling bookcase suitably filled with leather bound books. He was pleased to see a substantial fire burning merrily in the fireplace.

'Your bedchamber and dressing room are through here, my lord. I have assigned Robert, who assists his lordship's valet in his duties, to take care of your needs until your own man arrives.'

Mrs Johnson dipped a curtsy and vanished through the servant's door, cunningly concealed in the wooden panelling leaving Simon alone to survey his accommodation. It was as luxurious and well appointed as the rest of the house. He felt he should remove his dirty boots before crossing the Persian rug that filled the centre of the room.

His bedchamber door opened to reveal a young man with a shock of red hair and a beaming smile. 'I am Robert, my lord. If you come this way I shall soon have you looking smart again.'

In less than half an hour he was redressed in freshly pressed and sponged britches, spotless topcoat and his boots polished so well he could see his reflection in them. His host had had the foresight to provide him with a fresh cravat, so he left the room feeling refreshed and ready to hear the worst.

The footman who had conducted him to his rooms was waiting outside to lead him back. 'Lord Bryson is waiting in the study, my lord. I am to take you straight there.'

Simon half smiled, indicating he was more than ready. The butler stepped forward as he reached the hall and he was escorted by both men. He was accustomed to being treated with deference but was beginning to feel uncomfortable being paid so much attention.

'Lord Orpington is here, my lord,' the butler announced.

Simon stepped through the doors and bowed to the man standing, legs apart, a slight frown upon his face. 'Lord Bryson, thank you for your hospitality. I had expected to find Mrs

Sinclair at the Dower House.'

'No doubt you did, Orpington. But your bird has flown.'

Lord Bryson did not sound in anyway apologetic. In fact the man was viewing him with distinct disfavour. Simon felt his cheeks flush. What did this man know about the situation? How much should he tell him? He shrugged. Honesty was called for now, the time for prevarication and deceit was over.

'I have come down here to offer marriage to your sister. From your demeanour I take it you do not approve my suit.'

Lord Bryson did not offer him a seat, a sure sign that he was being viewed with opprobrium.

'Orpington, I must inform you that Sir Edward Dalrymple called at the Dower House yesterday. Mrs Sinclair is fully cognizant of your disgraceful scheme to entice her into inappropriate behaviour in order to gratify your propensity for gambling.'

Simon swallowed. He had not realised Dalrymple had heard the whole of
the conversation. 'You are correct to see
me as a villain, Bryson. However when
I made those reprehensible remarks
I had not understood my feelings
towards Mrs Sinclair. It was only when
I saw her lying unconscious, her head
resting in a pool of blood, that I realised
I loved her.' He rubbed his hand across
his eyes brushing away the tears as he
recalled the horrible image. 'Damn it,
man, I am not offering out of duty, but
out of love. Without your sister by my
side my life will be empty indeed.'

'Well said, Orpington. Come, sit
down before you fall. I could not
believe a man of your integrity could
behave in such a reprehensible way.'

Simon felt himself guided to a chair
and he sank gratefully into the soft
interior. He closed his eyes, resting his
head against the back of the chair,
marshalling his thoughts. Perhaps all
was not lost after all. If Bryson
supported his suit then maybe he could

persuade Patience to listen to him. He felt a glass being thrust into his hand.

'Here, drink this, it will restore you.' He heard Lord Bryson seat himself.

He sipped his drink, allowing the fiery cognac to warm his bones and steady his hands. He smiled grimly. It had taken a woman to reduce him to a quivering wreck — something Napoleon's finest had never achieved.

'I take it Mrs Sinclair has removed herself deliberately in order to avoid receiving my offer?' He sighed heavily. 'I shall not rest until I have convinced her of my love. Where is she? I must go to her immediately.'

'Not today, Orpington. Your horse needs to rest overnight and you and I need to get to know each other. After all we are to be brothers by and by. I am not at all like my sister; no doubt you have noticed my hair is blonde not red. I take both my character and my looks from our mother. My sister gets her temperament and colouring from our father.' He grinned, suddenly, making him look years younger. 'If ever a girl was misnamed it was my sister. My father was famous for his wit.'

Simon relaxed. He rather thought he was going to like this man in spite of their inauspicious introduction. 'You still have not told me where your sister has gone?'

'She has gone to visit Aunt Elizabeth who lives in Bath. They are travelling slowly and intend to make at least four stops; you will easily overtake them on that horse of yours, even though they have a two-day start.'

'Good God! Why should they wish to go to Bath at this time of year?' He chuckled. 'I suppose it was the furthest she could go without actually leaving the country to avoid me.'

'You have a deal of fence-mending to do, Orpington, before Patience will forgive you. Now do not look so dispirited — she will have you. She would not have been so distraught on discovering your perfidy if her own affections were not already engaged.'

They were disturbed by a discreet tap on the door and the entry of the butler. 'A light repast has been served in the small dining room, my lords. Her ladyship regrets she is unable to join you but will be down for dinner.'

'I do not usually eat mid-day, Orpington. However, today I find myself famished. Emotion plays havoc with a fellow's digestion.'

'Indeed it does, sir. I broke my fast so early this morning I have forgotten what I ate.' Chatting companionably the two men strolled through the house to share a luncheon, Simon liking the serious young man more and more as the day progressed. By the time he departed the following morning they were best of friends.

★ ★ ★

Three days after they left Ipswich, the travelling carriage from Bryson Court was still fifty miles from Bath. Patience had enjoyed the journey up till now, but the weather had worsened and a blizzard was blowing around the carriage.

'We shall have to seek shelter at the first coaching inn we discover, Mama. We cannot continue in this storm.' Patience let down the window and a blast of icy snow filled wind whisked through. Holding on to her bonnet she leaned out to talk to Sam who was riding alongside. 'Sam, how far is it to the Plough where we have rooms reserved for tonight?'

'We'll not make it there today, ma'am. But if I remember rightly there is a tidy establishment less than a mile from here. I shall go on ahead and arrange for our accommodation.'

She watched him ride off, his caped coat spread out behind him like a blanket to protect Othello from the worst of the elements. Her horse had survived far worse in the mountains of Spain. He would come to no harm; however the four bays pulling the carriage were not made of such stern stuff. The sooner they were in a warm stable eating a hot bran mash, the happier she would be.

'Shut the window, my dear, I am becoming more like a snowman than your mama.'

Hastily Patience regained her seat and pulled the window closed. 'I apologise, but it was necessary to speak to Sam. Did you hear what he said?'

'That there is a suitable establishment not far away. That is excellent news. If we all have to share one room so be it. Anything will be better than remaining outside in the snow.'

In fact the mile to the inn took longer than anyone had anticipated. The road was almost impassable, the snow swirling into deep drifts that made their progress slow. When, eventually the carriage turned into the cobbled yard the horses were done.

Sam appeared at door, looking like a white bear, and let down the steps for them. 'Thank the Lord you're here safe and sound. I reckon you'll be the last to get through until it thaws. The baggage arrived sometime ago and your rooms are being prepared and your trunks are already upstairs waiting for you.'

Patience realised they might well be forced to spend several days at The Queen's Head. She prayed that no one was stranded on the road behind them. In the severe weather conditions it was unlikely they would survive until help could reach them.

Inside the landlady, one Jenny Tims, was waiting to greet them, her cheery red face a welcome sight. 'Come in, your ladyship, Mrs Sinclair; your maids are waiting upstairs in your chambers. You're lucky, many of my expected bookings are unlikely to arrive and I have been able to allocate rooms to you.'

A tiny maid in a clean white apron and mob cap curtsied politely then led the way up the twisting wooden staircase to the first floor, upon which their rooms were situated. She stopped in front of a heavy black wood door and lifting the latch led them inside.

'This is your private parlour, my lady. I'm afraid you will have to share it with Mrs Sinclair.' She took them across the warmly carpeted boards and opened the door that led into the first of the bed-chambers. 'This is the best room — it has a dressing room leading from it and a truckle bed there for your maid.'

The room was clean and smelled of fresh beeswax and lavender. 'This is ideal for you, Mama. I shall take whatever else they have to offer.'

'If you would come this way, madam, I shall take you to your chamber. It is not so grand, but nice and cosy and leads on to the parlour as well.'

Patience was more than satisfied with the room. 'Does my man have a room inside?'

'Yes, madam, he has a small chamber in the attic. Is there anything else I can get you? There is already hot water and a tray will be arriving any minute. I expect you are sharp set, it is a long time since breakfast.'

The two ladies had just finished their repast when Mary exclaimed loudly. 'Good heavens, I do believe someone has just arrived. The poor horse is up to his hocks in snow and the rider is no better.'

Patience joined her at the bay window which overlooked the yard. 'I think the man must have been leading the horse for you cannot distinguish his britches from his boots. Can you see that he has placed his coat over the horse to protect it? How many gentlemen would care for their animals so well?'

She stood watching as an ostler fought his way across the yard to take the exhausted horse. There was something familiar about both animal and rider. She rubbed a clean space on the tiny leaded pane and jammed her face to the cold glass. Surely she was mistaken? How could Lord Orpington be here?

11

Patience felt her knees wobble and was forced to sit on the window seat to recover her composure. She wanted to race down stairs and fling herself into his arms thanking God that he had not been frozen to death out there in the blizzard. But she could not do this because he was nothing to her. He was merely the son of her godmother and a virtual stranger to herself.

'Madam, are you unwell? You've gone a mite pale.' Mary stood over her, her face anxious.

'It is Lord Orpington.' She finally managed to say. 'He is downstairs. He has ridden through the blizzard to find me.'

'Well I never! Once a soldier always a soldier. A bit of snow wouldn't hurt a man who followed Wellington all over Portugal.'

Patience shook her head. 'Should I go down or wait here for him to find me? I suppose that I must speak to him after he has made so much effort. But I have not changed my mind, Mary. I shall not marry a man who offers out of duty. Jack loved me and I loved him. I could not settle for a union without love.'

'You'd best smarten yourself up, ma'am. You don't want to be seen looking travel weary.'

'No, I shall remove my cloak and bonnet and wash my face and hands. No more. Lord Orpington must take me as he finds me. I did not ask him to seek me out after all.'

An hour had passed since she had seen his lordship stagger through the front entrance and still he had not asked to speak with her or even sent a message to say he had arrived. Patience was no longer calm, she was angry.

'Mama, if Orpington has come to see me why has he not announced himself? It is the outside of enough to keep me waiting like this.'

Lady Bryson attempted to smooth matters. 'My dear, have you considered that it might not have been Lord Orpington? And if it was, he would not know that you were gazing from the window at the precise moment of his arrival.'

'Good heavens! How silly I am being. You are quite correct I do not even know for sure that the figure I saw was Orpington. What is the matter with me? Whoever it is, they would need to bathe and change before being fit to visit anyone.'

She flopped down on to the chair nearest the fire feeling she had, as usual, overreacted. How was it that the very mention of his name could make her behave like the veriest ninny? She stretched out her legs to the warmth and forced herself to relax.

'I shall not send down to ask at the desk, Mama. I do not wish anyone to know I was gawping out of the window like a child. If it was Lord Orpington he will seek me out when he is ready and if it was not, then I am still happy that the gentleman arrived safely.'

* * *

As the snow worsened Simon began to fear he had overestimated both his strength and that of his horse. He had had no idea where he was on the road — all he could see was blinding whiteness. The biting wind and driving snow would kill Rufus if he did not do something to prevent it. He had no choice. He dismounted and removing his riding coat he threw it across his mount praying it would be sufficient to protect the stallion until they could find shelter.

'Come along, old fellow, I shall plod beside you. We shall soon be warm and safe and out of this blizzard.' Even as he spoke he knew that if they did not find an inn they would both be meeting their maker.

The faint yellow glimmer of the

lanterns swaying crazily outside the inn was like a godsend. He led his exhausted mount through the snow shouting loudly for assistance. A wizened ostler fought his way round from the stables to greet him.

'Here, sir, let me take the beast. You get yourself inside into the warm. I reckon God was on your side today — another half-hour and you would not have found us in this blizzard.' The old man was forced to shout against the howling of the wind to make himself heard.

'Thank you. Do whatever it takes to make my horse comfortable.' Simon put his shoulder to the heavy oak door and pushed almost falling into the vestibule. The cloud of snow that followed him made the candles flare and smoke.

'Leave the door to me, sir. You get over to the fire and get yourself warmed up.' The burly landlord grabbed the banging door and forced it to shut. Simon heard the bolts being rammed home behind him. It was the sound of this that made him realise just how lucky he was. As the ostler had said — half an hour longer and it would have been all up for him.

His legs were stiff, his boots caked with snow. His coat was no better. In fact, as his teeth began to chatter, he realised he was frozen to the marrow, that all his garments were wet and needed to come off.

'Landlord, I am in desperate need of a hot bath and dry clothes. Do you have a room available and some garments I could borrow until mine are dry? My valet is travelling separately. God knows where he is.'

'There is a tub being filled as we speak, sir. We have rooms spare for some of our customers have been forced to overnight elsewhere. No, sir, leave on your boots, a little snow won't hurt the boards.'

Simon knew his strength was ebbing. He had been out too long. He knew that he should have stopped at the previous hostelry but his determination to catch up with Patience had forced him to continue. He prayed, not something he was over-used to doing, that she had taken refuge somewhere out of the snow. If he should lose her now his life would be over.

'In here, sir. I shall send my son, Ned, to attend you. You need to get those wet clothes off and into the bath before you catch your death.'

Simon was unable to answer. He was clenching his teeth in order to stop them from chattering. He scarcely felt the rough hands of the landlord's son stripping him naked and half lifting him into the hip bath standing in front of a roaring fire.

Slowly the warmth of the water began to thaw out his icy limbs and his teeth stilled in his head but his tongue felt thick in his throat and his normally sharp brain was not functioning. He closed his eyes, aware that something was wrong but not sure what it was. From a distance he heard the young man speaking to him, but was unable to answer as he slipped into the blackness.

* ★ *

Upstairs Lady Bryson and Patience had finished their impromptu meal and declared it more than adequate.

'If the food remains as good as those pasties and the vegetable soup we have just eaten, our stay here will not be so bad,' Patience told her mother.

'And the rooms are clean and comfortable. I know how you hate to be kept inside, my dear, but we shall not be able to continue our journey until the snow clears. It is unusual to have such harsh weather in these parts. We are just unlucky to choose to travel at this moment.'

The curtains had been drawn across the windows an hour since and it was fully dark outside. Patience had nothing to occupy herself with apart from the book she had brought with her. Restlessly she wandered back and forth across the room.

'Mama, I am going downstairs to enquire as to the welfare and identity of the gentleman who arrived earlier.' She turned to her maid who was stacking the dirty crockery on the tray. 'Mary, come with me. I do not wish to be seen unaccompanied in a public place.'

Carrying their candlesticks aloft they followed the winding passageway back to the stairs and descended towards the noise and bustle of the public rooms. Mrs Tims, the landlady, was emerging from the snug as Patience reached the vestibule.

'I have come to discover the name of the gentleman who arrived a few hours ago. He looked familiar to me.'

The woman's face creased with worry. 'Madam, we have no idea who he is and he is too sick to tell us. My Ned is with him but his condition worsens by the hour and we cannot send for the physician with the weather as it is.'

'Mrs Perkins is a competent nurse

and so is her husband.' She turned to Mary. 'Would you and Sam take care of the traveller? I have my bag of herbs and medicines upstairs.'

'I should be happy to help. If you are sure you can manage without me. I shall come and collect your bag and then go to the gentleman.'

'No, Mary, you find Sam and go at once to the sick room. I shall bring the bag to you.'

Patience hurried back upstairs her heart thudding heavily. She prayed that the gentleman lying ill was not the man she loved. If anything happened to Simon she would be bereft — lost in a life with no meaning.

She burst into the parlour startling her mother. 'Whatever is the matter? You look so pale, has something dreadful happened?'

'Mama, that man who arrived on horseback is very sick and Mary and Sam are going to nurse him. I have come to collect my medicines and take them to the chamber he is in.' Not waiting for her mother to protest she dashed into her bedchamber to collect the bag and rushed out again.

The landlady had explained the whereabouts of the sick gentleman and she had no difficulty discovering the chamber for herself. She knocked on the door with shaking hand. She heard hurrying footsteps and Mary appeared. She did not have to ask. One look at her face told her all she needed to know. Ignoring all the rules of propriety she stepped past her maid and ran to the bed.

Her heart shrivelled as she surveyed the man tossing and moaning in his fever. It was Simon. Had she come too late? She dropped to her knees beside the bed and clasped his burning hands.

'My dear, if I had known it was you I would have been by your side all day. Whatever bad feeling there is between us is forgotten. I love you and pray that you shall recover.' Her tears dripped on to his fingers adding to the slickness of his perspiration.

'Madam, you must come away. Sam and I will take care of him. We have to strip him in order to reduce his fever and it would not be seemly for you to be here.'

For a moment Patience was tempted to refuse. She wanted to be the one to sponge him down, to spoon the special draught, made from the bark she carried in her medicine bag, into his parched lips. Slowly she pushed herself upright. 'I shall wait in my parlour whilst you take care of him. Call me if there is any change. I shall not retire to my room tonight.'

'I'll do that, ma'am. Leave his lordship to us. We know what we're doing and have done this many times before. He looks bad, I'll admit, but he's a strong man and has everything to live for.'

'Thank you, Sam. Remember, the slightest change and I wish to know.'

Patience turned to glance back at the figure fighting for his life on the bed. All she could do now, was pray. Mary and

Sam must do the rest. She returned to her own chambers to give the bad news to her mother.

'Oh my dear, how dreadful. But think how much worse it could have been.'

Patience lifted dull eyes to stare uncomprehendingly at her mother. 'How could it be worse? The man I love is lying at death's door along the corridor.'

'He could have been frozen to death outside. He could have remained untended. Child, can you not see? He is here and so are you and he has Sam and Mary to take care of him. That is a miracle in itself.'

'It is a strange coincidence, no more than that. I do not intend to go to my bed tonight, Mama, I must remain awake in case I am needed.'

'Then I shall stay awake with you.'

* * *

Patience was dozing uncomfortably in the chair on the right of the fire when she heard a quiet knock on the parlour door. She jolted awake but did not call out, her mother was asleep on the day-bed and she did not wish to disturb her. She hurried to the door dreading what news was awaiting her outside. A small boy greeted her.

'You must come at once, madam. I have been sent to fetch you.'

She followed the boy along the passageway accompanied by the sounds of snoring and coughing behind closed bed-chamber doors. At three o'clock in the morning most people were asleep. She did not ask why she had been sent for. She could not form the words.

On arriving at the private parlour that adjoined Simon's room she walked straight in. Mary was waiting for her.

'Madam, the fever has broken; Lord Orpington is out of danger. He is sleeping peacefully now.'

'I must see him for myself, Mary. I shall not be able to sleep unless I know he is safe.' She entered the bedroom and walked across to the sleeping figure. Sam stepped back at her approach.

'He'll be right as rain in a day or two, Mrs Sinclair. I'll sit by him all night so you can get some sleep.'

Patience, ignoring his comments, sat on the edge of the large bed. She needed to feel for herself that Simon was no longer burning up. She smoothed her fingers across his forehead and his skin was cool. She leaned forward and placed a gentle kiss upon his forehead.

'Sleep well, my love. I shall return to talk to you in the morning.'

To her amazement his eyes opened and he smiled up at her. 'My darling, is it you? Or are you a fantasy come to taunt me?'

'It is I, Simon. We shall talk tomorrow, my love, when you are better. I must return to my room.'

A surprisingly strong hand gripped hers. 'No, sweetheart, stay here with me. I shall not rest unless you are by my side.'

Patience heard the shocked murmur from behind her. She knew she shouldn't do so, she would be totally ruined, her reputation in shreds, absolutely compromised. She kicked off her slippers and swung her legs on to the bed. She giggled.

'If I am to share your bed tonight, my lord, you will have to marry me in the morning.'

'I have a special license in my coat. We shall be wed as soon as a priest can be fetched.'

Her face was radiant as she slipped her legs under the coverlet. 'Then there is nothing to worry about.'

'Mrs Sinclair, forgive me but I think this is a bad idea,' Mary said wringing her hands in distress.

'Do not fret, Mary, nothing shocking is going to take place. I wish you to remain in the room with us for the remainder of the night. But nothing in this world is going to take me away from the man I love.'

And nothing did.

We do hope that you have enjoyed reading this large print book.

Did you know that all of our titles are available for purchase?

We publish a wide range of high quality large print books including:
Romances, Mysteries, Classics
General Fiction
Non Fiction and Westerns

Special interest titles available in large print are:
The Little Oxford Dictionary
Music Book, Song Book
Hymn Book, Service Book

Also available from us courtesy of Oxford University Press:
Young Readers' Dictionary
(large print edition)
Young Readers' Thesaurus
(large print edition)

For further information or a free brochure, please contact us at:
Ulverscroft Large Print Books Ltd.,
The Green, Bradgate Road, Anstey,
Leicester, LE7 7FU, England.
Tel: (00 44) **0116 236 4325**
Fax: (00 44) **0116 234 0205**

Other titles in the
Linford Romance Library:

DEAR OBSESSION

I. M. Fresson

Dr. Manley's wife Kate has allowed her son Johnnie to become an obsession, excluding the rest of her family. However, when the doctor takes a new partner, Dr. Paul Quest, everything changes. Johnnie becomes more independent and her husband less willing to go along with her obsession. Kate, now realising that she is in danger of losing her husband, must also accept the bitter truth: that Johnnie is capable of doing without her . . .

ALL TO LOSE

Joyce Johnson

Katie Loveday decides to abandon college to realise her dream of transforming the family home into a country house hotel and spa. With the financial backing of her beloved grandfather the business looks to be a runaway success. But after a tragic accident and the ensuing family squabbles Katie fears she may have to sell her hotel. When she also believes the man she has fallen in love with has designs on her business, the future looks bleak indeed . . .

ERRAND OF LOVE

A. C. Watkins

Jancy Talliman flies halfway around the world to Bungalan, in Australia, to renew an interrupted love affair with Michael Rickwood, who she'd met in London. She remains undaunted on discovering that he's unofficially engaged to Cynthia Meddow, especially given the support of Michael's brother Quentin, and his sister Susan. Jancy settles in a small town nearby. Then as she becomes involved with the townspeople, dam worker Arnulf, and Quentin, Jancy alters the very reason for her long journey south . . .